Twisted Together

The Chronicles of Kerrigan, Volume 8

W.J. May

Published by Dark Shadow Publishing, 2016.

D1607711

This is a work of fiction. Similarities to real people, places, or events are entirely coincidental.

TWISTED TOGETHER

First edition. February 12, 2016.

Copyright © 2016 W.J. May.

Written by W.J. May.

G

Also by W.J. May

Bit-Lit Series
Lost Vampire
Cost of Blood
Price of Death

Blood Red Series
Courage Runs Red
The Night Watch
Marked by Courage

Daughters of Darkness: Victoria's Journey
Huntress
Coveted (A Vampire & Paranormal Romance)
Victoria

Hidden Secrets Saga
Seventh Mark - Part 1
Seventh Mark - Part 2
Marked By Destiny
Compelled
Fate's Intervention
Chosen Three

The Chronicles of Kerrigan
Rae of Hope
Dark Nebula
House of Cards
Royal Tea
Under Fire
End in Sight

Hidden Darkness
Twisted Together

The Chronicles of Kerrigan Prequel
Christmas Before the Magic

The Hidden Secrets Saga
Seventh Mark (part 1 & 2)

The Senseless Series
Radium Halos
Radium Halos - Part 2
Nonsense

The X Files
Code X
Replica X

Standalone
Shadow of Doubt (Part 1 & 2)
Five Shades of Fantasy
Glow - A Young Adult Fantasy Sampler
Shadow of Doubt - Part 2
Four and a Half Shades of Fantasy
Full Moon
Dream Fighter
What Creeps in the Night
Forest of the Forbidden
HuNted
Arcane Forest: A Fantasy Anthology
Ancient Blood of the Vampire and Werewolf

The Chronicles of Kerrigan

Twisted Together

Book VIII

By

Copyright 2016 by W.J. May

The Chronicles of Kerrigan

Chronicles of Kerrigan Prequel

A Novella of the Chronicles of Kerrigan.
A prequel on how Simon Kerrigan met Beth!!
AVAILABLE:
.99cent for a LIMTED TIME

Find W.J. May

Website:
http://www.wanitamay.yolasite.com
Facebook:
https://www.facebook.com/pages/Author-WJ-May-FAN-
PAGE/141170442608149
Newsletter:
SIGN UP FOR W.J. May's Newsletter to find out about new
releases, updates, cover reveals and even freebies!
http://eepurl.com/97aYf

Description:

Twisted Together is the 8th Book of W.J. May's bestselling series, The Chronicles of Kerrigan.

Rae Kerrigan has been branded a traitor.

Arrested with no idea why, Rae suddenly finds herself on the wrong side of the Privy Council and possibly for good. She's branded a traitor, just like her father.

Forced to trust in someone she doesn't know, she finds herself more confused than ever. Gabriel is cocky, brash, distractingly handsome and apparently working for the Privy Council under Carter.

Forced to prove her innocence, Rae will stop at nothing and risk everything.

Twisted Together is the 8th book in the Chronicles of Kerrigan series.

Book 1, Rae of Hope is currently FREE.

Follow Rae Kerrigan as she learns about the tattoo on her back that gives her supernatural powers, as she learns of her father's evil intentions and as she tries to figure out how coming of age, falling love and high-packed action fighting isn't as easy as the comic books make it look.

Series Order:

Rae of Hope

Dark Nebula

House of Cards

Royal Tea

Under Fire

End in Sight

Hidden Darkness

Twisted Together
Mark of Fate
Strength & Power
Last One Standing
Rae of Light
Prequel: Christmas Before the Magic

Prologue

Put a big bird in a small cage, it will sing you a song.

- **Patrick Watson**

Chapter 1

Not this bird.

I cannot BELIEVE this is freakin' happening.

You know that dream you have when you finally come home after saving a bunch of people from a psychopath...only to be arrested in front of your mom, your boyfriend, and all your friends?

Yeah...I was pretty much living that.

"You have to let me out of here. Eventually!"

Rae shook back her long raven hair. It was straight today, falling in silky waves down her back. A purposefully formal look, paired with a lavender dress, intended to impress and appease the host of adults waiting for her back at the Privy Council.

Under the present circumstances, it was unbelievably annoying.

She spat out an accidental mouthful of abusive words, at the same time pounding her hands on the door. "I know you can hear me! What the heck?! I don't even get a phone call?!"

A harsh silence followed her words. She listened as they echoed into the darkness of the tunnels beyond her cell, growing quieter and quieter every time until there was just...nothing.

"You have got to be kidding me," she mumbled to herself, cursing as she tottered back and forth on the uneven stone floor in her high heels. As she took them off and conjured herself something more feasible for imprisonment, she took in her surroundings for the first time.

When the guards had first escorted her down here, she had been too shaken to notice much of anything going on around her.

This couldn't really be happening, could it? They weren't actually, really, having her *arrested*, were they?

She had put up absolutely no resistance, and trailed behind her guards like she was attached by a string, moving as if she was floating rather than walking. She didn't see the dank stone walls, didn't notice the occasional drips of water as they led her deeper and deeper beneath the foundations of the school and Privy Council buildings. She had no idea what was above her, what direction they had gone, or even how long they had walked. She was even too preoccupied to notice she was in handcuffs.

Instead, her mind was filled with a stilted montage of faces; a dozen different faces, each of the best people she knew. Each staring at her in muted horror as she was carted off in unbreakable chains.

Devon's face, in particular, stood out to her. Handsome as ever, but pale—literally frozen with surprise; his dark chocolate eyes wide with wonder and then anger.

As usual, he and she seemed to be on exactly the same page. When the guards had sprung up from nowhere and grabbed her arms, he looked like he thought it had to be some kind of joke. After all, they were technically standing in the middle of the safest place in the world. In the very heart of the Privy Council, surrounded by family, teachers, and friends.

Who the hell in that room would mean any of them harm?

He had made an impulsive movement when they led her to the door, taking an automatic step as if he meant to either stop them or follow, but Julian's hand had flashed out quicker than lightning and held him firmly in place. Whatever was going to be done to stop this, it wasn't going to be done right there in that room. There were larger forces at play.

As for the rest of them, Molly and Julian, her two best friends, wore identical expressions of bewilderment. When Carter did nothing to stop the guards, Molly had actually started to smile, unable to believe it could be real, while Julian's face had turned uncharacteristically grim. Her instructors and the rest of the PC faculty averted their gaze, literally looking anywhere else to avoid seeing what was happening. Carter's face had been unreadable, but she was sure she had seen shock in it before he covered his emotions. Even Devon's father, a man who had up until recently historically hated her, seemed to be having trouble meeting her gaze.

That just left one face left. And in many ways, it was the hardest one to bear.

Her mother's.

Beth alone didn't have a split-second's doubt about what was happening. She must have known what was coming from the start. Her face was lined with worry, and tight with pain from the moment Rae had walked through the door. In fact, it was her troubled eyes that had cued Rae in to the fact that anything was wrong to begin with.

Then she had turned her shocked attention onto Carter, the man in charge of everything.

Once things had begun to click into place, she automatically turned to him, along with the rest of her friends. Carter would make things right. As the President of the Privy Council, not to mention a personal friend of the family and one of the few people in the world who knew what Rae and her friends had really been up to this last month, there were few doors he couldn't open, few messes he couldn't get them out of. Surely he wouldn't let Rae be *arrested* the second she walked through the door.

Except... he stood by just like the rest of them.

His face was stern and unreadable as two strong men she had never seen before led her away into the dark.

AND FOR WHAT?!

The unfairness of the situation hit her all over again and she stormed back to the door, using the tatù of her old mentor, Jennifer Jones, to maximize the noise.

Rae was out there *for them*! For the damn Privy Council!

One could even argue she was out there because of them!

If they weren't so stymied by their own narrow-mindedness, then none of the hybrids she had been racing all over the world to save would have been in hiding in the first place. At the first sign of danger, they could have come straight to Guilder for help and protection. Instead, they were living on the run, in a perpetual state of hiding from the one organization that had sworn to protect them. But no, the Privy Council had literally decided to ban them from existence; leaving them easy prey for the likes of Cromfield. Not that they Privy Council was in charge of the entire world, but still...

Rae huffed in frustration.

And then there was Cromfield himself.

For the last four weeks, Rae and her friends had been working tirelessly against him, risking their lives every day, sticking their heads in the crosshairs to save the lives of the innocent. They'd walked away from everything they knew, everything that was waiting for them after graduation.

Their cushy government jobs, their new penthouse apartments, their friends and family—all to fight a villain that the Privy Council had yet to even acknowledge existed. And now Rae was being arrested for it, like *she* was the threat.

Her fists actually left little craters in the hard stone as she beat against the door of her cell. "I know you're out there, I can *hear* you—you freaking mouth-breathers! Are you even going to let me know what I'm being charged with?!"

The answering silence did nothing but fuel her rage. She beat the door still harder, shivering slightly in her thin dress as she rattled the bars of her temporary cage.

"All this funding and you guys still don't believe in centralized heating?" More pounding. "In case you didn't notice, I'm a teenage girl. I can keep this sort of thing up all day. So you should just let me out already—"

There was a deep groan from the iron lock, and the next second, the door pushed open.

"Finally," Rae took a step back in relief, "what took you so...?" She stopped short at the look on Carter's face. It was not the look she had been expecting: The dependable, infallible protector she'd come to know; the constant peripheral security blanket she'd come to rely on without even realizing it before this very moment.

The moment it was taken away. Forever.

"You're not here to let me out...are you?" Her voice grew small and frightened without her permission, and she dropped her eyes quickly so Carter wouldn't see them fill with angry tears.

Instead of answering, he shut the door firmly behind him, listening for a moment to make sure they couldn't be overheard before turning back to face her. "No, I'm not here to let you out." He looked as distressed as she had ever seen him. A whirlwind of conflicting emotions was held in check by only a very thin layer of control.

Unfortunately, that did nothing to ease her panic. "I don't understand why this is happening." Her voice shook as it rose in volume. "I found Cromfield, for Pete's sake! I found his secret hideout; I saved a list of people from his crazy little designs. I have freaking proof! Why the hell am *I* the one being arrested?!" She wanted to add, 'what about the others' but bit her tongue. She wasn't going to drag her friends into this mess... Unless they were already being questioned and arrested as well. *So help me, if they are...*

Carter's eyes flashed. "Miss Kerrigan, if you expect me to come in here and have a conversation with you, you will at least do me the curtesy of *lowering your voice.*"

"*Miss Kerrigan?*" Rae repeated softly. "What happened to 'Rae'?"

Carter's face tightened, then hardened all at once. "I'm not here to let you out," he repeated flatly. "I'm afraid, in that matter, my hands are tied."

Rae's eyebrows shot up in disbelief. "*Your* hands are tied? Mr. President?" It was hard to ignore the irony. "I still don't even know what I did. Is this all because we took off for a month and didn't tell—"

"This isn't about last month; it's about what you did at graduation," Carter interrupted harshly. His eyes flicked almost nervously to the door, and he dropped his voice down half an octave. "Your little demonstration in the Oratory."

Rae's mind blanked in confusion. "Little demonstration...? I was told to do that. It wasn't like it was an optional thing. Everyone in my whole class had to go in there and—"

"Except no one in your class did even half of what you were able to do. While a few of the alumni were simply impressed, you absolutely terrified the members of the Council. They looked out at you and saw nothing but your father. That day was Simon Kerrigan all over again. It was exactly what everyone who was nervous about letting you into the school was afraid of."

It felt like a cold hand was squeezing around Rae's heart. Without thinking about it, she fell back a step, struggling to find herself in the aftermath of those terrible words. "But I work for the Privy Council..." she murmured, staring at him with wide, disbelieving eyes. "After everything I've been through these last years—working to help—how can they still doubt my intentions? How can they *still* see my father, when I've proven I'm nothing like him?"

For the first time, Carter's eyes infinitesimally softened. "Simon Kerrigan had one of the most powerful abilities the Privy Council had ever seen. To this day, he remains, in their eyes, the biggest threat to our way of life to date." He paused uncomfortably. "Until you."

Rae's temper flared up. "But I haven't done anything—"

"But you *could*. That's their whole point. Your tatù puts Simon Kerrigan's to shame, and you're only beginning to fully develop your powers. There's no telling what could happen in the future, what way your alliances could turn."

"And they don't think that imprisoning me here might be exactly the way to make that happen?" she demanded, bringing herself up to her full height. "I freaking *work* for them."

"And *that's* why you're here," Carter growled. "If you had just been a private citizen, it might have been different. But when you disappeared for a month, certain members of the Privy Council were able to paint it as an agent 'going rogue.' They said they couldn't have such a potentially dangerous person within the government heading off on their own. It gave them exactly the excuse they needed to put you in here and throw away the key."

And throw away the key...

Rae shivered and took another step back, folding her arms protectively across her chest. She remembered what Devon had said about people getting put into holding just because of the potential hazards of keeping them free. Mrs. Lachaise had called it 'getting disappeared.'

Right now, it felt like a little of both.

In a moment of chilling clarity, she was struck with a sudden thought she never, in a million years, thought would have ever crossed her mind.

I should never have come home.

"Aren't you afraid I'll just break out?" Her eyes flashed, catching what little light there was in the cell, and she took a sudden step forward. "If I'm such a powerful threat, a potential hazard to your entire way of life—what makes you think I won't just walk right out of here?"

Carter glanced again toward the door before lowering his voice to a hoarse whisper. "That is precisely what you cannot do! You cannot justify what they're saying about you."

"That's easy for you to say—"

"I'm not the only one saying it." He took a breath and tried to collect himself. "Your mother sent me here to give you that exact same message. This is something to be dealt with from the outside. You are absolutely forbidden to go anywhere."

"This isn't being grounded! This is jail!!" Rae threw her hands up in frustration, unintentionally breaking the cuffs that had somehow survived her incessant pounding. She winced apologetically as they clattered noisily to the ground, and Carter flashed her a pained look. But it was that very look that got her temper up again. "Don't you even want to hear about what's been going on this last month? We found Cromfield's—"

"To be honest, Rae, I'm more worried about you right now."

Of everything that had happened that day, it was those words that made Rae come up short. Those words made her realize how serious this really was.

If Carter was more worried about what was going to happen to her than he was about Jonathon Cromfield, that was bad news. The worst.

"Just...sit tight," he said quickly. "And don't try anything. I'll be back when I can." He was out the door before Rae had a chance to say another word. The iron lock clicked loudly behind him.

Rae heard him conversing softly with the guards stationed down the hall, and then all was quiet once more.

For the first time in years, she found herself burying her head in her hands, taking deep breaths like her therapists had taught her to do all those years ago to help manage her lingering trauma about the fire that supposedly killed both her parents.

She sank down against a wall, bringing her arms up around her knees and clutching them tightly to her chest.

*It's not real, it's not real...*she found herself chanting. More tricks of the trade, meant to nip her panic attacks in the bud. Except, this time, she couldn't be more wrong. It felt like the prison room Lanford had put her in years ago. She mimicked the breathing she learned when she was a kid, after her parents died.

This is real. This is as real as it gets.

She didn't see another soul for the rest of the day. When a tray of cold dinner was pushed through the wall several hours later, it was done so by a pair of gloved hands that vanished as quickly as they had appeared. She picked miserably at the food, which looked to be some sort of vegetarian casserole, before deeming it inedible and pushing it angrily to the side. Instead, she tried to conjure up some fish and chips, a little comfort food to calm her down. But after taking her first bite, she spat it out into the plate and shoved the whole thing back through the slit in the wall.

Molly was right. She should stick to drinks and clothes. She had yet to make any sort of food that didn't trigger an automatic gag reflex.

Tiny tears sprang into her eyes as what felt like the weight of the world came crashing down on her shoulders. Her throat tightened up and she bit down hard on her lip, but she forbade herself to cry. If there was one thing she wasn't going to do down here, it was cry. She made the promise to herself the second she walked through the door.

Instead, she made herself a mug of piping hot chamomile tea and tilted her head back to the ceiling. The room where they were keeping her was as basic as it got: A simple cot surrounded by four walls of stone and a stone ceiling. But there was a little barred hole cut through the rock about fifty feet up that allowed her a small glimpse of the night sky.

It was here that she focused her troubled eyes, wondering vaguely what prisoners were supposed to do when it rained. She was still mulling that one over when she conjured herself a thick blanket and drifted off into the rockiest of slumber.

If Rae was expecting some sort of end-of-incarceration miracle the next day, she was sorely disappointed. Aside from another tray of what looked to be 'swamp' for breakfast, she didn't see a single person. They were assuredly banning all visitors, she thought as she watched the sun travel from one side of her little ceiling hole to the other. That was why no one had come.

She hoped her mom was giving Carter pure hell for this. She hoped her friends were doing the same to the rest of the Privy Council. Her thoughts grew almost smug as she imagined it:

Beth, the love of Carter's life, tearing him a new one for arresting her daughter. Devon, the golden boy of the Privy Council, threatening to quit unless Rae was released.

She wondered what sort of future Julian was seeing for her now. With so many different people and factors in play, it was probably clouded beyond his sight. And what about Molly? She had officially graduated from Guilder; was she already staying in their new apartment? Was she there right now, moving everything in while her best friend sat in jail? If she was down here for a long time, would they begin to move on without her? Like she didn't exist?

Those tears threatened to come again, and Rae quickly switched her attention to something else. They insisted on confining her here? Fine. Then she would stay.

But that didn't mean she couldn't make a few desperately-needed improvements...

An hour later, Rae was kicking back on a giant plush love seat. It had been shoved into the corner, next to her king-size bed. A host of colorful little cups of espresso lay scattered on the coffee table before her, complementing the color of the obligatory Monet replica hanging on the wall. She had even gone so far as to conjure up a simple television, and was just contemplating how she'd go about replicating cable when there was a deep groan, and the door pushed open again.

Carter blinked in amazement as he stared around the cluttered room.

It looked like something out of the pages of 'Home Design.' At least, that's the image Rae had had in her mind when she conjured it. And it couldn't be more ridiculously out of place, juxtaposed against her present location.

"This is..." he stuttered furiously, "what the hell is..."

For one of the few times in his life, he was actually so thrown by what was in front of him that he couldn't find the words to speak. Then his eyes fell on Rae, sitting smugly in the middle of it, and he suddenly found the words after all.

"Rae Kerrigan!"

"What?" she asked innocently. "I'm *here*, aren't I?"

She wanted to add, 'and good luck getting the bed out that door,' but she didn't think it would be the best idea to push Carter any farther than she obviously already had.

"They told me Guider needs a new headmaster," he was mumbling to himself, pacing in furious circles and tripping over a Persian throw rug. "What could be more of a delight, living with a bunch of rowdy teenagers with superpowers?" His eyes flashed up to Rae and she wisely kept her tongue. "I came to tell you that your situation here is permanent until further notice." He spoke loudly, and his voice echoed off the walls of the tiny room. "You are to remain incarcerated until such time, if ever, that the Privy Council sees fit to release you."

Rae blinked. Then blinked again.

He wasn't kidding. She could tell that much. But he wasn't exactly looking at her either. His eyes kept flickering up to the hole in the ceiling, almost like he was waiting for something to arrive.

"I'm...going to stay in prison," she repeated the words slowly, unable to register something so completely insane. "How're you letting that happen?"

When Carter finally did look at her, he was a different man. Stiff. Cold. Like he was back in her first days at Guilder.

There was something else there as well. Something she couldn't quite place.

"I told you, Miss Kerrigan, it's out of my hands." He swept back towards the door, but paused before opening it, glancing back at her with an intensity she found almost as unnerving as the message he had come to deliver. "I can only hope that you mind what I'm telling you, and that you're still here in the morning. You're to be transferred to a more secure facility... One there's little hope of ever leaving."

Rae's mouth fell open and she stared at him in shock.

In the morning she was going to be moved to a permanent facility there was no chance of breaking out of? And Carter wanted her here for that? "What the hell is going on?!" she yelled.

"Like I said, Miss Kerrigan," he glanced again at the roof, and this time she followed his gaze, "I expect to see you here in the morning. Once you get to the new facility, it'll be too late."

A chill ran up her spine but she nodded slowly. "I...understand." They locked eyes and he gave her the slightest of nods. "I'll be here. Don't worry."

All at once, he was his condescending self again. "I never do." Without another word, he marched out of the cell, locking her inside behind him.

She stared at the door for a long time after he'd gone, replaying every word in her head, trying to make sure she had it right.

Carter was telling her to escape, right? He was saying that, come tomorrow morning, it would be too late, so she had to leave tonight.

Right?

Why the hell couldn't anyone here ever just speak plainly and say what they meant? Why didn't the PC know about Cromfield to begin with? Why was Rae the only one acting like a grownup in a world full of adults?!

She glanced down at her newly-conjured cupcake slippers and rethought that last one.

Nevertheless, she kept her ear to the door for the rest of the night. While no one dared to venture outside her actual cell, it sounded like there was at least one guard stationed at all times at the end of the hall. Rae glanced around the stone walls, and suddenly wished she hadn't made so much clutter. It would be easy enough to escape, that much was clear, but she wasn't sure how she was going to do it without making noise, alerting security.

She went over option after option in her head.

Transform into an eagle to slip through the bars in the ceiling? No, they were too close together; she'd never make it through.

Conjure up a giant ladder and literally walk her way up to the sky? No, she'd still have to deal with the bars when she got there. And while she could easily pull them apart with her bare hands, the sound that would make would also attract the guards.

She was still mulling it over, staring pensively up at the sky, when a shaggy head of blond hair suddenly popped into sight.

"What the—" She jumped back in alarm, squinting up to try to make out the identity of the person silhouetted against the moon. She didn't think it was anyone she recognized, not with that color hair, but it was a young guy; she could tell that from how he moved. Furthermore, he was clearly trying to be quick and discreet, constantly checking over his shoulder as he ran his fingers over the thick iron bars.

Or should she say...what used to be the thick iron bars.

The second his hands touched them, it was like the metal simply disappeared.

Finally rid of the only thing that stood between her and freedom, she ditched all her previous plans and literally ran up the stone walls, swinging her body over the ledge and landing on the ground beside the guy who was responsible.

The...um...very *hot* guy who was responsible.

Rae couldn't tell if she was blushing, or if she was just flushed from the run. But she took a second to collect herself before looking up into a pair of sparkling green eyes.

"Who are you?" she asked quickly, lowering her voice to a whisper as she glanced nervously around. "What're you doing here?"

"Isn't it obvious?" his voice was sparkling too, as light and mischievous as his smile. "I'm here to rescue you."

Chapter 2

"You're here to rescue me?" *Does he not know who I am?* Rae bit back a smile. "I really can't tell you how utterly clichéd that sounds."

His smile faded into irritation as he reached forward with a gloved hand and grabbed her wrist. "Whatever; alright, just take my hand and let's get out of here."

He jerked her forward, pulling her along a few steps beside him, before she planted her feet firmly in the ground. When he still tugged her a few steps further, she turned up a strength tatù.

"What the hell?" he hissed as he was jerked backwards. "We've got to leave—NOW!"

Rae crossed her arms firmly over her chest. She had been tossed back and forth in this magical world of superpowers and high-stakes missions enough times to get whiplash. Needless to say, she certainly knew better than to get swept off in a rescue with the first guy she met, handsome or not. If Lanford, Carter, Jennifer, and Angel had taught her anything, it was that you never knew what side people were playing for and what they could do. This guy had yet to let her touch his skin. For all she knew, he was a stunner just like Julian's crazy on-and-off-again girlfriend.

He certainly looks like stunner, she thought with an inner grin, but that's not exactly what she was worried about at the moment.

Rae settled her feet firmly shoulder-width apart as she realized she had been under Guilder and was now standing on the football pitch, or somewhere close by it. "Look, I don't know you. For all I know, you could be working for the Privy Council—trying to get me in even more trouble by breaking me free."

"I do work for the Privy Council," he said openly, "but it's not exactly what you think."

Rae threw up her arms and took a giant step back. "Are you freaking kidding me?"

"Get down!"

Before she knew what was happening, he'd tackled her flat to the ground, covering her body completely with his own. She blinked up at him in shock, feeling the warmth from his skin seep through her thin dress. The golden tips of his hair tickled the tops of her cheekbones, and for a moment all was quiet except the sound of their shallow breathing.

Run, Rae—run! Push this gorgeous guy off of you and head for the hills.

But something about the way he was holding himself made her pause. There was a tension in his body that put her on high-alert... An alert that soared to even greater heights as she switched to Devon's tatù and heard what this guy had obviously seen a second earlier.

A pair of heavy-booted footsteps. The Privy Council's guards, out on patrol.

She instinctively sucked in a panicked breath—a breath that smelled deliciously like citrus and aftershave—and held perfectly still.

To be frank, she didn't think she'd have been able to push her way past those muscled arms planted in the grass on either side of her anyway. She might not know much about this guy, but he clearly knew how to handle himself. And, as much as she hated to say it, he had clearly just saved her butt.

His green eyes flickered down to hers as the footsteps walking past them grew quieter and quieter before disappearing altogether. His lips were just inches away from her own, and as she drew in another silent breath, she could have sworn she saw him wink. Another scent of him filled her nostrils; as much as she wanted to hate the smell, it was intoxicatingly delicious. No one smelled this good. Not even Devon.

"I think it's safe to go now, but I'd be perfectly willing to stay here another couple minutes if you prefer..."

Rae pushed him off of her, sending him flying back several feet before he landed with a soft chuckle in the grass. She'd switched to Jennifer's tatù almost immediately after hearing the guards, lingering on Devon's for only a moment. She didn't know quite how to explain it, but she felt almost...guilty, using Devon's ability while lying beneath some other guy. "Look, I don't know who you are, or what you think you know about me, but I guarantee that out of all the girls I'm sure you've used that line on in the past—I'm quite capable of taking care of myself." She stood and brushed a handful of leaves from her lavender dress. "For the record, you didn't have to tackle me; I would've been just fine."

The guy leaned back on his arms, grinning without shame as his eyes gave her a lengthy once-over, from the tips of her shoes to the tips of her hair. "Well...I'm wearing black. It's good color for a late-night rescue mission, you know. And you're wearing..." his eyes swept over her again, lingering in a way that made her blush, "...well, *that*. So I figured it would be better if I was on top."

A rush of blood blossomed in Rae's cheeks and she turned away furiously, trying to get her bearings whilst completely ignoring the arrogant Adonis lounging on the ground beside her.

"Okay, okay." He got to his feet, putting his hands boldly on her shoulders. "Next time, you can be on top."

The next second, he went flying backwards again. His blond hair stood straight up on end, and little curls of smoke trailed from his jacket.

Rae flashed him a bitchy smile. She had always loved Molly's tatù. It was one of her favorites.

"Wow..." He shook his head with a little grin, walking cautiously back towards her. "He told me you were feisty, but—"

"Who told you I was feisty?" she demanded.

The time for games had passed. Each second they stayed out in the open was a second they could get caught. She needed answers, and fast.

For once he seemed to understand the need to be serious, and his face sobered up as he stared intently into hers. "Carter."

Her eyebrows shot to her hair. "*Carter* told you that? You expect me to believe that you're working for Carter?"

"That's what I meant by: I technically work for the Privy Council, but it's not what you think." There was the sound of a door opening and closing, and without seeming to think about it, he grabbed her hand again, pulling her down beside him into a crouch. "Look, I understand why you're a little jumpy, you just got arrested and all, but we can discuss all of this later? Right now, we've got to get out of here."

She yanked her wrist away with a vicious tug. "I can get out of here all on my own, thanks. I'm not going anywhere with the likes of you."

He pursed his lips and stared back at her with a mixture of frustration and amusement. "I know you've been searching for Jonathon Cromfield for the last month with your friends. I know he's after a list of hybrids and you've been trying to keep them safe. And I know that when you spoke to the headmaster tonight, he told you—point blank—to run."

Rae's breath caught in her chest. There was absolutely no way he could know all of that. Not unless...

"Fine," she hissed. Couldn't Carter have sent her a different rescuer? One without...dimples? Devon had one. This guy had to have two. "See if you can keep up."

Without a second glance behind her, she darted silently across the lawn, staying in a low crouch and keeping to the shadows. She could feel the internal battle waging in her body, as it tried to decide which tatù would be most effective: invisibility or speed. She settled on speed, mostly because, while it would obviously help not to be seen, she could still be heard. And she happened to know of at least three working members of the Privy Council who were gifted with super hearing. In the long run, it was probably just better to get off Guilder grounds as quickly as possible.

That was bad news for mystery guy, who was having trouble keeping up.

With a stifled sigh, Rae circled around and came up behind him. "What the heck? Carter didn't think to send me someone with a useful ability for this sort of thing?"

"My ability is plenty useful," he panted, glaring as he sprinted across the grass. "As for you, why don't you just turn into a bird or something and fly on out of here?"

Rae bit her lip as she flushed with automatic embarrassment. She had thought of that too, obviously, but her brilliant eagle shift came with one unfortunate consequence: it left her without clothes. Choosing not to reveal this little hiccup, she urged him forward. "Someone has to stay behind to save your ass," she dodged his question rudely and pointed up ahead. "There! That's the main gate."

"Yeah, I know," he snapped back, clearly annoyed. "I went to this crappy Ivy League- worthy school too."

They both slowed down slightly as they approached, staring nervously ahead at the guards and cameras. Since when were there guards at the gate entrance? *Since the PC locked me up.*

Rae didn't know exactly what it was, but there was something different about the entrance to the school tonight. She'd driven this road a million times, and she was sure of it: something was definitely off. Her eyes flicked all around the forested lane, its old-fashioned street lamps giving the entire thing an almost-picturesque glow. They had managed to run through the forest line beside the school and twin tower entrance. She squinted at the gates.

What was it? What was going on?

That's when she saw it: A little shimmer in the air above the iron gate, almost too faint to see, but most definitely there. Her eyes grew wide as she saw that it wound around the perimeter of the entire school.

"What is that thing?" she whispered, pulling her companion to a stop. "In the air, what—"

"It's kind of like an anti-tatù force-field. It keeps people with abilities from coming in and from going out. It's why we couldn't get away through any other part of the school."

Rae's face tightened in confusion. "And why's that, exactly?" If this thing didn't allow for the use of powers, she didn't see why they were trying to escape at all. They were trapped.

It's probably exactly what my would-be prison cell is lined with.

All at once, something squeezed her hand. She looked up in surprise to see the guy standing very close to her, staring into her eyes with a soft, calming encouragement.

"Hey, calm down. I can feel you freaking out all the way from here, okay?" He squeezed her fingers again, and, for the first time, she didn't pull away. "We came to the main gate because it's the only part of the school that isn't protected. They had to take down the shield to allow the cars of the people who actually work and go to school here."

Rae nodded quickly, eyes darting nervously to the three PC guards standing before it. They had what looked to be not only the standard Tasers the rest of them used, but actual guns as well.

In a sudden flash of illumination, she realized that she had actually never wondered about Guilder's security before. She'd always vaguely supposed that a virtual castle filled with people with super powers didn't need much protection from the outside world.

Now, standing on the wrong side of their little magical fence, she was beginning to rethink that.

"So what are we going to do?" she asked nervously. If she used Jennifer's tatù, she could take down the guards and pry apart the bars of the gate before anyone was the wiser. In fact, if she just approached from the—

WHAT THE HELL?!

Before Rae could make sense of what was happening, both guards were on the ground. Her mystery man had come out of nowhere, taking both of them down in a blur of speed like some sort of James Bond. He hadn't used an ability—he'd only used his hands—but Rae had been through enough combat training to know that it took a special kind of talent to do what he'd just done.

When he'd finished, he turned back to her with a huge grin. "What we're going to do," he ran his fingers over the iron bars, and, just like before, they seemed to melt away at his touch, "is walk right out of here."

Rae's jaw fell open and she stood there in shock. "Who the hell are you?!"

"Gabriel Alden... nice to meet you." He extended his hand as if jail breaks were the most natural thing in the world, and pulled her gently through the open gate.

A little spark buzzed through her skin as they touched, something she wasn't sure was entirely to do with her mimicking ability, but she chose to ignore that possibility. Sure enough, she could already feel the telltale buzz through her skin as the new tatù settled in with the rest.

She glanced up quickly to see that he was watching her closely.

It must be strange, she thought, although it was something she was so used to, she rarely remembered. *It must be so strange to watch someone else take an ability that was uniquely yours.*

"Do you have it?" he asked quietly. There was an odd note of strain in his voice, almost as if he regretted giving it away.

"Yeah, um," she cleared her throat awkwardly, "I do. You can manipulate metal..." she murmured, feeling it out. She was surprised by the potency of it. "And it's...*very* developed." Her eyes fell on his face inquisitively, suddenly wondering how old he was.

He shook his head with a low whistle, clearly impressed. "You know," he put his hand on her back and began leading her down the street, "I know about a million people who would love to get their hands on that fairy of yours."

There was a hitch in both their steps, and his cheeks blushed furiously. "That..." he laughed nervously, "definitely came out wrong."

She forced herself to laugh as well, before pulling discreetly away. Something about the words were hitting a little too close to home. "It's fine."

A car with tinted windows started heading up the drive, and she pulled him quickly into the shadows, ducking behind some low-hanging trees. They watched with bated breath as it rounded the curb and vanished from sight. Just a moment later, it would be at the gate.

...and would see the two disabled guards.

Rae's heart fluttered nervously in her chest and she turned back to her rescuer with impatient, expectant eyes. "Well, you wanted to be my knight in shining armor. What comes next?"

"Next?"

He raised his eyebrows mischievously and pulled her further into the trees. They kept walking for another minute until they came to a little side road Rae had never known about before. Parked right in the middle was a black sports car; something she didn't know the first thing about, but she was sure would have made both Julian and Devon drool.

"Next, we go for a little ride..."

By the first hour, Rae had snuck enough looks at the gorgeous Gabriel to have memorized his face perfectly. It was the kind of face you didn't see walking around on the street. It belonged in a magazine or on some billboard for the latest blockbuster. His long lashes framed eyes so green they were almost startling, and his perfect bone structure traced down to a pair of lips that...

But Rae was very much in love, so she was determined not to notice those sorts of things.

You can't help but look, a little voice told her. *It's not like you like the guy. He's just undeniably attractive, that's all.*

By the second hour, it was very clear that Rae most definitely did not like him. Gabriel may have been good-looking, but he knew it, and he was smug. There was a constant cockiness that was incredibly off-putting and an arrogance about his skills that made Rae want to go one-on-one with him in the Oratory and wipe that smirk forever off his perfect face.

Not at all like Devon, that same little voice chimed in. Devon was just as hot as this guy, some might even argue hotter, but he didn't wear it on his sleeve. He was modest and kind. The perfect boyfriend. Perfect...in a lot of things.

By the third hour, Rae was starting to realize that they were quickly leaving England behind.

"Where are you taking me?" she finally demanded, staring out the window at the black, star-studded sky. The landscape all blurred together, and considering she had never had the greatest sense of direction to begin with, she had absolutely no idea where they were.

Gabriel looked up with a little grin. "Scotland."

Scotland?!

Rae tried to keep it together, leaning back in her chair and trying to act as casual as him. "Naturally..."

Not ten minutes later, they pulled onto a side road that led down to the darkened sea. Rae's eyes grew wide as they climbed out of the car, and she pulled her coat tighter around her as the frigid salty air bit into her skin.

Before her lay what looked like the ricketiest, most unstable, most unseaworthy excuse of a boat she'd ever seen in her life.

"Please, *please* tell me we're not going on that," she whispered, leaning into Gabriel so as not to offend the giant man who was wandering down the wooden planks to meet them.

"Of course we are," he answered cheerfully. "Petey's a good friend of mine. And, while he usually uses this thing to catch mackerel, he said he'd give us a ride to Scotland, free of charge."

Her eyes flickered again to the ticking time-bomb. It was bobbing up and down on the choppy sea, like a bath toy that had reached the end of its rope. One good wave was sure to do it in.

"What," Gabriel smirked down at her, "are you scared?"

She glared. "Well actually, I've seen *Titanic*, so, yeah... I am... a little."

"Relax." Ignoring her protests, he pulled her into a tight, one-armed hug. "I'm not going to let anything happen to you."

On most any other day, she would have shoved him firmly away and shown him just exactly how relaxed she could be. But between the freezing gusts of wind and the spray from the icy waves crashing up against the hull, she actually nestled in a bit closer, taking full advantage of the heat radiating off his body.

How was it that boys always ran so hot, she wondered absently as he spoke in low tones to the fisherman. *Must be all that annoying testosterone...*

"Alright," Gabriel turned to her with a small smile, tightening his arm as he looked down at her pink nose and chattering teeth, "he says we can stay below in the main cabin. Doesn't want a little thing like you to catch your death of cold." He winked.

"Whatever," Rae muttered, bracing herself against the chill. "Let's just get inside, okay?"

He led her down the narrow stairs, steadying her when she slipped on the slick wood, and pushed open the door with a grand relish. "Our chamber awaits..."

'Chamber' was a bit generous. There was one bed, pushed into the center of the room, with not much space for anything else. A small thick-paned window above the mattress steamed over the second they walked inside, but Rae could still hear the sudden onslaught of heavy rain just outside.

"*Our* chamber?" she repeated, raising her eyebrows.

If she was hoping this statement would make a difference, she was sorely mistaken. Gabriel was already taking off his thick jacket and the sweater beneath, leaving him in nothing but a tee-shirt that hung deliciously on his muscular frame.

"Yes," he grinned as he hopped onto the bed, "*our* chamber. You don't expect me to sleep outside, do you? And, I hate to say it, but there's not much room on the floor."

Rae glared, but it didn't seem like there was much she could do. She followed suit, slowly removing the wool trench coat she'd conjured on the drive over, before coming to pause at her dress. The silk was wet almost all the way through, clinging to her skin in a way that made her turn quickly around, trying to tune out the way Gabriel watched her every move with a sly smile.

"Do you mind?" she finally asked, crossing her arms tightly over her chest.

He leaned back against the headboard, folding his hands behind his head. "Not at all."

Her eyes narrowed in a warning. "I have a boyfriend, you know. One that you and your little metal magic don't really compare to."

The room filled suddenly with his loud laugh. A happy sound, despite the undertones that ran beneath it. "Oh, Rae...you clearly don't know me at all."

The words hung between them, and, after a second of blatant shock, Rae couldn't help but smile. This guy had *absolutely no shame*. None at all! It was unbelievable.

Still shaking her head, she held out her hands and conjured a thick down duvet. Even the almighty Gabriel couldn't hide his surprise as she spread it carefully on the bed, snuggling down under the covers as far away as she could get.

Once she was settled, she glanced over her shoulder in false concern. "Oh, I'm sorry—did you want something?"

The threadbare comforter on the mattress couldn't provide much any heat.

"Well, actually I—"

"—Guess I just assumed you had your ego to keep you warm." She grinned into the pillow, proud she had cut him off just at the right moment.

Those were the last words either of them said until morning.

Chapter 3

When bright morning light streamed in through the window, Rae moaned, and brought her hands up to her eyes. A part of her couldn't believe she'd actually fallen asleep on this dilapidated monster of a boat. Another part couldn't believe the thing had made it through the night in one piece.

"And she finally opens her eyes," a superior-sounding, incredibly sexy voice said from somewhere over her shoulder. "Well, good morning, princess! Turns out you wanted to share that blanket after all."

Wait...*what*?

A pair of warm arms tightened in a circle around her waist, and Rae let out a gasp of shock.

Somehow, in the night, she and Gabriel had ended up spooning in a warm cocoon under her down comforter. Her back was nestled snugly against his chest, while the rest of her body was cradled tightly in his strong arms. She could feel the tip of his chin resting on her hair, and, just to increase her humiliation, even their legs were comfortably intertwined.

"What did you do?" she accused, struggling valiantly against his arms.

"Me?" The arms tightened playfully and she felt his warm breath by her ear. "If I recall correctly, it was you who scooted over here when the storm picked up. You know," a pair of long fingers curled a loose strand of hair behind her ear, "you're a lot nicer when you sleep..."

"Get the heck off of me!"

In hindsight, the strength tatù was poorly-timed. The second she slipped into it was the same second he chose to let go. What resulted was a magnificent fumble in which Rae sent herself flying not only off the bed, but into the opposite wall.

She hit the wood with a soft crunch, sliding slowly down to the floor as her pale skin bloomed red in furious humiliation.

"Careful," Gabriel chimed in cheerfully, sitting up with the sheets wrapped around his waist.

Rae pulled herself to her feet, prepared to finally let him have it, when she stopped short in disbelief. "Where is...why are you...?"

Only Gabriel's triumphant smile could have made her angry enough to pull her attention away from his bronzed, sculpted abs. *"Why the hell did you take off your shirt?!"*

"What? Oh—this?" He gestured down to his bare chest with a wicked smile. "I got hot in the night. You were cuddled in so close...I couldn't wear it a second longer."

Rae was beside herself. The NERVE of this guy! As if it was something she'd want. As if they weren't in the process of fleeing the country. And after she'd *specifically* told him that she was already seeing someone.

"Calm down, sweetheart. It's not like I took my pants off—"

"Oh...that's bloody it!!!"

A second later, he was cowering on the other side of the room—clutching the blanket around himself as he raised his hands up like a shield.

"Rae! Rae, think about this! I really can't stress enough what a bad idea it is to create an electrical storm when we're out on the open water!"

Damn science! It had to work against her every time!

Rae lowered her smoking hands to her sides, but her dilated eyes locked onto his, keeping him standing straight at attention. "Let me make this perfectly clear." Her voice was dangerously low. "You do not touch me, *ever*. You do not, for a second, take this lightly. This is my *life* we're talking about. This is my freedom. And let me assure you, blondie, I'm not remotely interested. So why don't you take a breath, remember that you were sent here for a reason, and go find out where the hell we are?"

For once, Gabriel didn't talk back. He simply gave her a quick jerking nod before skirting around the bed to get to the door.

He was almost outside when she rolled her eyes and called, "And Gabriel?"

He paused, a nervous hand on the frame. "Yeah?"

"Put your damn shirt on."

When she finally joined him on the deck about ten minutes later, he seemed determined not to acknowledge the awkward power struggle in the slightest. He hardly gave her a second glance as she walked past him and the captain, putting her hands on the icy rail and gazing out to sea.

She'd finally ditched the lavender dress and conjured herself something new—something a bit more appropriate for the weather. The wool trench coat was stylish and fitted, patterned off something she'd seen in one of Molly's magazines, but it was still far and away the warmest thing she owned. She'd paired it with some matching amethyst gloves and tall suede boots. Since she was in no rush to see Gabriel again, she had even thrown in a little cap to match.

Molls would be proud, she thought as she stared out at the waves. *She always says purple is one of my best colors.*

"Good thing you took off that dress," Gabriel said quietly as he joined her.

She threw up her hands in exasperation. "Do I have to just toss you overboard or—?"

"I *meant* it's going to be below freezing today. The last thing I need to explain to Carter is why you went hypothermic and lost two of your toes." He raised his hands innocently and offered her an appeasing smile. "Honest."

Something about his coaxing yet unapologetic face made her almost smile back in spite of her better judgement. It was hard to stay mad at someone who was so completely unashamed of their actions. No matter how infuriating it might be, there was a playful stubbornness behind it that had to be almost admired.

Nevertheless, she kept her composure as she turned her eyes back out to the ocean. "That better have been what you meant," she mumbled, but she flashed him a begrudging grin. "Did we really *have* to take a boat, anyway?"

"Well, all the roads are being watched, so, yeah," he flashed a quirky smile that reminded her a little of Devon, "we *had* to take a boat."

She turned away guiltily, wondering how, if ever, she could explain to Devon what exactly happened last night. She was worried it might be one of those, 'you'd totally get it, but you'd have to have been there' sorts of things...

The two of them watched in silence as the little fishing craft pulled up to a dock, half-hidden beneath a bank of tall grass. Once they were close enough, the captain, Petey, jumped out and hitched a rope over a sunken log, before tugging the boat closer with his bare hands.

"Does he...?" she paused curiously. "Is he inked too?"

Gabriel shook his head with a faint grin. "No. He's Scottish."

After thanking Petey profusely, the two of them climbed into yet another black sports car that was waiting for them on a little dirt road near the water. As Rae strapped the seatbelt around her, she glanced at Gabriel curiously. He seemed just as in his element here, in the middle of farm country, as he did on the streets of London. And as he did on the fishing boat, for that matter. She wondered where it was he came from, where had he developed that confidence and all those skills. He was young, probably just a few years older than her, but there was something aged about the way he looked at things. It wasn't necessarily wise; it was aged... deep behind those sparkling eyes of his.

"So I've narrowed it down to two things in my head," she started conversationally, gazing out at the endless fields of green, trying to avoid staring too long at the guy beside her. "We're either going to a Braveheart reenactment, or you brought me out here because you have a secret affinity for sheep."

He snorted but kept his eyes on the road. "Neither. Both. It's even worse than you imagine."

She grinned and turned back to the window. "Seriously, Gabriel, what's going on? If Carter told you to break me out of jail, wouldn't he want you to take me to my mom? My mom who is back in London? Why the hell did he want us to come all the way out here?"

"Because everyone in London is being watched." He suddenly pulled off the road, down a lane that was barely visible through the tall grass that surrounded it.

Rae sat up higher in her seat and noticed they were headed to what looked like a farmhouse sitting in the center of about a million acres of rolling hills, except it wasn't a farmhouse at all. It was way too big for that. It looked more like some sort of residential-style Scottish resort than anything else, sitting pretty as a picture against the golden glow of the rising sun. There was even a little barn in the back.

"What is this place?" she asked in awe, pressing her fingers against the window. It was beautiful, and the image tugged at her as if she had seen it before. Maybe in a painting or picture?

Gabriel glanced at her for a moment before answering. "Everyone in London was being watched," he repeated, "so they all came out here."

They pulled up into a gravel driveway beside a row of familiar-looking cars. Rae's heart leapt in her chest as she saw Julian's Jaguar, her mother's old Lexus, and Devon's over-the-top sports car—whose name he always told her but she always forgot.

"They're here!" she half-squealed, not bothering to hide her enthusiasm. It felt like years since she'd seen her friends, even though technically it had only been two days.

Prison ages you, she thought sagely as she leapt from the car, not bothering to wait for Gabriel.

The door was unlocked and she rushed inside, pausing for a moment to savor the heat and look around excitedly at the old-fashioned kitchen. There was a well-worn wooden table in the center, surrounded by a compliment of mismatched chairs, accompanied by a stack of old recipe books piled precariously atop an oven permanently coated in what looked to be tomato soup, and an old wood-burning stove that sat chugging away in the corner.

Rae loved it! It was exactly the cozy, homey atmosphere she missed from childhood, and secretly craved.

She was about to ask how exactly her little troop of degenerates had ended up here, but a low buzz of voices from above sent her tiptoeing up the stairs. There was a light on at the end of the hall and she paused behind the door, peeking through a crack in the wood.

She almost laughed aloud.

The place was set up like a war room. There was a huge chalkboard at one side, covered with what looked like a detailed map of the Guilder grounds, and piles of books and diagrams spilled off the oak table onto the floor.

Devon stood at the center like a drill sergeant, hitting the board repeatedly with a long stick as he lectured on and on about security. Molly and Julian were sitting on two chairs pushed up against the wall, looking stressed but bored. Heaven knows how long they'd been sitting there.

Finally, when she couldn't take it any longer, Rae cleared her throat. "So...who are we rescuing?"

The room went instantly quiet—for about three seconds.

"Rae Kerrigan!!" Molly flew off her chair in a blur of crimson, little sparks flying behind her as she launched herself at her friend.

If Rae hadn't already been well-accustomed to her exuberance, she might have fallen over, but fortunately she knew to brace herself just in time.

"What on earth are you doing here? We were just coming to break you out!" Molly pulled back and looked her anxiously up and down. "Did prison change you? Have you taken up smoking? What was the food like? You didn't try conjuring anything yourself, did you? We all know how bad you are at that. That's a great jacket by the way—"

"Back off a minute and let her breathe." Julian smiled warmly as he walked forward, literally lifting Molly off her feet and setting her aside so he could give Rae a tight hug. "It's good to see you," he murmured. "How the hell did you break—" He waved his hand as if it didn't matter. She was *Rae Kerrigan*. "I can't believe they took you away. I've been trying to keep an eye out for what's going to happen, but—"

"Don't worry. I'm okay." Rae beamed, shaking her head. "I figured it would be too..." Her voice trailed off as her eyes fell on Devon.

For a moment, the two of them just stood there, staring at the other like they were lost in some sort of dream. Then she was in his arms.

"I am so, *so* sorry that happened to you," Devon whispered roughly into her hair. For once, it was him crushing her, but she didn't really mind. She just held onto him, grinning like an idiot and soaking it all in. "I missed you so much, Rae—I was so worried. I swear I'm never letting you go again."

"I certainly hope this is the boyfriend," a loud voice announced from behind them.

Rae turned around with a grimace as Devon looked up in surprise.

Gabriel stood leaning in the doorway, a playful smirk dancing on his face. "Otherwise I'm afraid that's terribly inappropriate. Dude, you should see how she was with me!"

"Who the hell are you?" Julian asked sharply from the corner, looking the new guy up and down with obvious dislike.

Gabriel peeled himself away from the door frame and strode forward. "Oh, I'm sorry, how terribly rude of me not to introduce myself. I'm Gabriel. Gabriel—"

"—Alden," Devon finished flatly. "I know who you are." He turned to Rae in surprise. "What's he doing here?"

An incriminating flush spread up Rae's neck, and she bit her lip. "Actually, it's kind of a long story. You see, Gabriel was the one who—"

"I got her out," Gabriel interrupted. "Busted her out of the Guilder Detention Center, while you guys were sitting around here just talking about it; saved her ass, protected the package, you know, all that jazz." He glanced at the chalkboard with a sarcastic little smile playing about his lips. "Nice drawing, by the way."

Devon's eyes flashed and he took a sudden step forward. "Listen, it's not like—"

"I'm sorry," Molly cut him off, wandering over to Gabriel and looking him up and down with wide eyes—eyes just as shameless as his own. Once she was finished, she turned to Rae with a girlish, conspiratorial grin. "Um...whoa."

Rae rolled her eyes. "Yeah, I know." Gabriel flashed a cocky grin behind her and she continued, "And trust me, he does too."

"Wait," Julian was still putting two and two together, "Gabriel Alden..." He shot Devon a questioning glance, and Devon nodded with a rather pained expression. "You're the guy who was hired by the Privy Council?"

"Just three months ago." Gabriel clapped him cheerfully on the shoulder, purposely ignoring t when Julian pulled deliberately away. "Already risen up the ranks to 'senior informant.' You know, I can't be sure about this," he leaned back against the table and shot Devon a bright smile, "but I'm pretty sure I climbed the ladder even faster than the golden boy over here. Imagine that."

Devon forced a tight smile. "Imagine that."

Again, Molly butted in. "But if you work for the Privy Council and are so high up, why on earth would you help Rae break out of jail? Aren't you supposed to be on their side?"

Gabriel grinned widely. "Well, our dear Rae is right—it *is* a long story. And it all starts with this little lavender dress—"

Casting all pretense aside, Devon blurred across the room with the supernatural speed of his ink. His hands had balled into tight fists, and, judging by the look on his face, he was about to end Gabriel's little ladder-climbing once and for all.

However, whatever was going to happen between the two no one would never know, because at that moment the door pushed open once more.

The five teenagers turned as one to see the pale, tear-stained face of a beautiful woman in her early forties. A woman who happened to look very much like Rae.

"Mom!" Rae breathed, rushing towards her.

Much to her surprise, Beth caught her by the shoulders and held her at an arm's length, looking her up and down as if unable to believe it could be true.

"Rae?"

The next second, both mother and daughter were in a bone-crushing embrace. Rae's shoulders relaxed in relief as she rested her head on her mom's shoulder. She hadn't realized how shaken up she'd been by the last forty-eight hours until this very moment.

Of course, there was the previous month to consider. A fact that, unfortunately, hadn't escaped Beth's notice either. She took Rae by the shoulders and pulled back again. They were the same height, but somehow there was something in her mother's eyes that made Rae feel about two feet tall.

"Well now that you're out of *jail*...you have a lot of explaining to do, young lady."

Rae's eyes slid behind her mother to a picture on the wall. She stared at it for a moment. Was that her mother... and Uncle Argyle?

"Rae, pay attention." Her mother moved, blocking Rae's view of the old photograph of two young kids.

Thankfully, the international road-trip recap took a lot less time than Rae had imagined. Her friends, who had gotten to Scotland two days previously, hadn't been so lucky. Rae assumed from a lot of her mother's long-suffering sighs and already-answered questions, that she'd probably spent the last forty-eight hours interrogating each and every one of them.

"I still don't know why you didn't tell me," Beth said for the twelfth time. They were perched on two easy chairs in the war room. The others had discreetly made themselves scarce. "I'm your *mother*, Rae. That's supposed to mean something."

Rae dropped her eyes down to her lap. There was an obvious answer here, but one that she absolutely couldn't say. Although it was through no fault of Beth's...Rae hadn't had a mother in a long time. "It *does* mean something," she said quietly. "It means everything—you have no idea. It's just that..."

With gentle fingers, Beth reached out and smoothed down Rae's hair. "It's just that you've been getting by on your own for a long time now. I'm sure it can't be the easiest thing to make room in your life for someone when you're so used to taking care of yourself."

Rae peeked up through her lashes. "He had to be stopped, mom. He was out there killing people just for...just for being like me. You were living at Guilder, under the protection—and therefore the surveillance—of the Privy Council, the very people who weren't supposed to know what we were doing. I couldn't tell you. I couldn't call you. And I didn't want to try to bust you out and take you along because..."

Her voice trailed off in embarrassment, but much to her surprise Beth simply laughed.

"What? Just say it, Rae. We both know what you're thinking."

Rae threw up her hands in exasperation. "Because I feel a little protective of you, okay? I lost you once, you know? I'm not exactly eager to repeat the whole ordeal."

Beth was still chuckling as she pulled Rae in for another huge hug. "While I admire this courageous side of you, I'm the one who's supposed to be protecting you. Not the other way around."

Rae rolled her eyes and grinned. "Haven't you heard the news? You probably need protecting from me. I'm, like, number one on the Privy Council's 'crazy' watch list."

Beth's face hardened and she took Rae's hand, helping her to her feet. "I'm afraid you're a bit more than that now. I'm afraid you're also, officially, a fugitive." She sighed as she led Rae downstairs to where the others were waiting in the kitchen.

The tension in the air was immediately clear. There seemed to be an unofficial line between Gabriel and the other three; a line that all of them, even Molly, seemed unwilling to cross. Beth saw it at the same time and sat down squarely in the middle at the kitchen table, gesturing for everyone else to do the same.

"Molly, Julian, Devon," she looked at Devon sharply as she said his name, "Gabriel here risked his life upon Carter's orders to free Rae from the Guilder Detention Center. He deserves our thanks, don't you think?" She cast Devon another pointed look.

Devon sighed quietly, before crossing the kitchen and extending his hand. "Thank you," his face was hard, but the words were sincere, "for what you did for Rae. Because she's my girlfriend, I'm sincerely grateful."

Beth sighed impatiently, and Molly stifled a giggle.

Gabriel merely grinned. "No problem, man. It looked like you were well on your way with your little tunnel drawing, but I figured someone had to step up to bat first." He gave Rae a devilish wink, and she rolled her eyes in disgust.

A muscle twitched in Devon's jaw but he tried to maintain composure. "We were all being watched. That's why we couldn't break her out ourselves. That's why we had to come here to Scotland to regroup and come up with some sort of plan." His expression grew suddenly smug. "It's also probably why Carter chose you: Because you're nothing to Rae. Who would suspect you?"

Gabriel smiled innocently. "Who indeed?"

A strange, heated implication hung in the air between them, and before tempers could boil completely over, Rae loudly cleared her throat.

"Moving on...where are we with Cromfield? Were you guys able to come up with any information as to his whereabouts?"

"In the forty-eight hours since we went to Scotland and you were carted off to jail?" Julian scoffed and then dropped his tone as he teased her gently, "Uh, no, Rae. We've been a bit occupied."

Rae was not to be deterred. "Well, we've got to get started. I think the best place to begin is to map out a list of everywhere we already know he's been: Dates, locations, activities. We've got to create some sort of timeline that we can—"

The front door swung open with a loud bang, and everyone sitting at the table whirled around in alarm.

"Actually, I may have an idea about that."

Chapter 4

"James!" Beth was up from the table in a rush of speed, darting over the rickety floor boards and throwing herself into Carter's arms without shame.

Rae gagged silently and returned her attention to the table, and even Carter looked a bit surprised to be on the receiving end of such an embrace.

He rested his hands lightly on Beth's back, looking like he could finally cross this moment off his bucket list, when Beth pulled back and gave him a kiss on the cheek.

"You got her out." She kissed him again, on the lips. "I knew you would."

"Whoa, wait a minute," Gabriel leaned over and whispered in Rae's ear. "Are Carter and your mom going at it?"

"*Ew*—no. Shut up, Gabriel," Rae snapped, rubbing his breath off her neck.

Carter cleared his throat self-consciously, at the same time seeming unwilling to physically let Beth go. He kept one hand on her arm, gently squeezing it as he replied, "Of course I got her out, Beth. I wasn't going to leave your daughter in jail."

So much for my daydreams of mom tearing him a new one for letting me be arrested.

Devon, Julian, and Molly seemed to be of a similar mindset.

"But you had no trouble whatsoever letting her get arrested in the first place," Molly said boldly, putting her hands on her hips.

Carter finally tore his eyes away from Beth and looked at the pint-sized girl in surprise. "I had no choice, Miss Skye. When there was nothing but radio silence from you lot for the better part of a month, certain allowances had to be made."

"Certain allowances like shutting Rae up in a cell?" Devon's eyes flashed as he looked his boss up and down. "She's a fugitive now, Carter. There's no going back. How could you let something like that happen?"

Carter stared around the little kitchen in alarm. This was obviously not the kind of welcome he had envisioned when he drove out here. "Now wait just one minute—"

"We trusted you," Molly said accusingly, bringing herself up to her full height. "When you said you couldn't tell the Privy Council what was really going on, but that we should all go out on this secret mission anyway, we trusted that everything would be okay when we came back."

"And you were right to do so!" A vein in Carter's neck started throbbing. "I don't think you understand the precariousness of the position I'm—"

"How were we right to do so, when the second we got back, Rae went to jail?" Julian asked softly. His dark eyes fixed on Carter's with a burning intensity that demanded the truth. "And don't tell me it was some big surprise for you. You're the damn president! You had to have purposely waited to make any permanent decision until the last second so I wouldn't see..."

Carter glanced helplessly at Beth, but in the end, he turned his eyes to Rae.

She was perched on the edge of her chair, keeping her eyes trained on the table. In the two days she was kept in holding, she had imagined screaming a great many of these exact things at Carter once she saw him again. But her friends beat her to the punch.

"Rae..." he began tentatively, sensing, or perhaps hoping, that if he got her forgiveness the rest would automatically follow.

She lifted her eyes with a little sigh, locking them on her old boss. She no longer worked for the Privy Council.

The same boss who had sworn to protect her. The same boss who had sent her off on this international goose chase to begin with. The same boss who then screamed at her in the tunnels underground, loudly pronouncing for all the world to hear how she had turned out exactly like her father. How she would spend the rest of her miserable, 'potentially dangerous' life in prison.

"Rae...do you understand why I did what I did?"

She stared at him quietly, not saying a word.

"If we want to catch Cromfield," he continued gently, "that's something we're going to have to do ourselves."

"Why?" she demanded quietly, curling her fingers in frustration. "We take all the risks and we're penalized for it? *I* go to prison, and *I'm* the threat? That's so unfair."

Carter sighed. "I know it is. But Rae, you've stumbled into the middle of a series of events that started long before you were born. Lanford had been working to undermine the Privy Council for the last three decades, slowly turning their already old-fashioned, conservative mindset to even more radical heights. Jennifer Jones had been passing information to Cromfield and slowly furthering his agenda since you were just a baby, and now I'm beginning to suspect that we may have yet another leak within the organization."

Everyone in the kitchen shared a quick look of alarm, and he sighed again.

"The point is that Cromfield has been working for countless years, not just to undermine the Council, but to do it from a place of absolute and utter anonymity. Trying to convince them that *he's* the one responsible for what's been happening since you started at school, instead of you—Simon Kerrigan's daughter—would be absolutely futile. They needed a villain, and you gave them one. To say anything different...I'd be fired on the spot just for suggesting it."

He saw the obstinate look on Rae's face and clarified quickly.

"And if I thought that might actually help, I'd do it in a heartbeat. But I'm of far more use to everyone if I stay exactly where I am now; keeping a grip on things as best I can."

Rae's eyes welled up with angry tears and she lowered them quickly to the table. "Even if it means I can never go home again."

In a flash, Carter was sitting at her side. He took her hand without seeming to even think about it, speaking with a fervor she had never heard before. "You *will* go home again. We *will* clear your name, and we *will* bring Cromfield to justice. I swear it. But, in the meantime, I'm afraid I have some other rather troubling news that requires our attention."

Much to Rae's surprise, he turned to Julian and Devon before continuing.

"It seems that one of the pieces of Simon Kerrigan's brainwashing device has gone missing."

The boys reacted with twin looks of shock.

Almost immediately, Julian sank into the nearest chair, his eyes glassing over as he surrendered himself to his visions, trying to get any piece of information he could.

Devon, on the other hand, glared at Carter like all of this was somehow his fault. "How the hell is that even possible?" he demanded, crossing his arms furiously over his chest. "When we scattered them, you assured us that—"

"I assured you that they would have the ongoing protection of the Privy Council," Carter finished for him. "And now I'm telling you that one of them has gone missing. It's the single biggest piece of evidence we have to support the theory of another leak."

"Wait a minute." Rae leaned forward across the table. "What on earth are you guys talking about? My father's brainwashing device? I thought the PC had it—"

"They did have it," Devon explained, still glaring at Carter, "until they ordered Julian and me to spend the better part of last year scattering it throughout Britain. And now..." his eyes flashed, "it appears that they've lost a piece. Or all of it..."

As if Cromfield needed anything else to give him the upper hand. Perfect! Let's give him a freaking brainwashing device...

Rae turned to Carter with a similar accusatory stare. "How many pieces are there?"

Carter rubbed his eyes, looking abruptly tired. "There are four.: Two of them are secure, Cromfield has already obtained one, and the fourth—"

"I can't deal this right now!"

The entire room turned around in surprise, Rae included, to see Devon pacing across the floor, wringing his hands like he was on the verge of some sort of panic attack.

What the hell?!

Rae pushed back her chair in alarm, trying to get his attention, but he completely ignored her, clutching the back of his neck as his shoulders rose and fell with his shallow breaths.

"This is too much! It's just too much. Rae was just arrested for following orders, we're trapped in a Scottish farmhouse, and now you expect us to go out on *another* mission? You must be out of your mind..." His eyes flicked almost imperceptibly to Julian, before he continued the pacing anew.

Carter's mouth fell open as his brow furrowed with concern. He shot Beth a bewildered look, but before he had the chance to say anything, Julian suddenly slumped down in his chair.

"I can't see *anything*!" He slammed his hands on the table in a most uncharacteristic loss of control. "There's too much going on. Everything's clouded! It feels like my skull's about to split open. I need to step back for a second, clear my head, get some air..."

His dark eyes shot to Molly, and Rae could have sworn he kicked her under the table. She certainly jumped abruptly in her chair before tossing back her long red hair, a sigh worthy of a martyr escaping her.

"Maybe you'd be able to see something if we had a freaking second to rest! Honestly," she exclaimed at the adults, "how do you expect us to keep going at this pace? I haven't slept in two days. There's no coffee. We haven't had anything to eat. I suffer from cripplingly low blood sugar, did you know that?"

Devon grimaced painfully at her performance, before he sank into a chair and turned to Beth and Carter in supplication. "Give us some time, alright? Some space. Beth, do you think we could get something for lunch? And it's freezing in here. Can't we turn on the stove?"

Beth's eyes widened in surprise while Rae discreetly bit back a smile. She didn't think Devon had ever asked Beth for anything. And as for the trio's little outburst?

Molly peeked at Rae from between her fingers and Rae took her cue. "I think I'm going to throw up. Or faint." She shuddered dramatically and lay her head down on the table. "Maybe both."

The entire room lapsed into stunned silence. The adults and Gabriel didn't know what to make of it. To see the Privy Council's four most independent, capable agents crumbling under the pressure like a bunch of, well, teenagers? It would have been comical if it weren't so damn serious.

Beth automatically sank down beside Rae, rubbing calming circles on her back, Carter was staring at Devon like his favorite toy had begun to backfire, and Gabriel was looking at the lot of them like they were crazy.

"Are you guys...are you serious right now?" he murmured, his green eyes sweeping over their defeated, crumbled posture in amazement. "What the hell happened to you all last month?"

"Beth, please," Devon groaned, covering his face with his hands, "can we get a little heat in here? I can't even focus. It's freezing."

"And some food?" Molly whimpered. "I feel like I'm going to pass out..."

"Of course!" Beth exclaimed, pushing to her feet and rushing across the room to the refrigerator.

"Bethany... *Now?*" Carter asked hesitantly. "I mean, we really need to talk about this—"

"Yes, *now*, James," she said through her teeth, re-diverting her worry into rage. "Can't you see we've been pushing them too hard?" She pulled out the contents for sandwiches and slammed them down on the counter. "Or should I say, *you've* been pushing them too hard. The most significant thing *I've* done in the last few years was get kidnapped and end up brainwashed."

With a mild nod of submission, Carter sank into the nearest chair, reaching tentatively towards Julian like he was going to pat him on the shoulder, but rethinking it and waiting silently for whatever was coming next. Beth was a blur around the kitchen, pulling things out of cupboards and yanking out plates before she suddenly whirled around on Gabriel with the same 'mother tone' she'd used on Carter moments before.

"And *you*! There's some scattered firewood on the far side of the barn. Go bring in an armful, would you?" She patted Molly soothingly on the head as she rushed by. "We're going to get this place heated and sort some things out, alright? No more mission talk. In fact, I'll put on some hot chocolate."

Gabriel backed away with wide eyes. "Yeah, I'll bring in the firewood, but..." His gaze swept once more over the kitchen before he shook his head. "You guys have fun with the...uh...talking about your feelings part, alright? I'll be in the car, catching up on some sleep."

A frigid gust of air swept into the room as he opened and closed the door, pulling up his hood as he marched across the frozen yard to the barn.

The second he was gone, the room transformed.

Devon sat down at the table as if nothing had happened. Julian yanked his phone out of his pocket and began casually texting, while Molly and Rae lifted their heads off the table and began calmly smoothing down their hair.

"Thank the Maker," Molly murmured. "I thought he'd never leave. But, uh..." she glanced curiously at Devon, "why did we do that again?"

"Yeah," Rae swept her hair up into a ponytail, "I'm up for a good nervous breakdown as much as the next girl, but why Gabriel?"

Devon purposefully ignored their questions, folding his hands instead neatly in front of him in an abruptly professional manner. "Back to business. We hid three of the four pieces on the west coast of Ireland, Wales, and—"

"Wait just a bloody minute!" Carter exclaimed, staring at the four of them like they'd gone mad. "What the hell's going on here?"

"We found our second wind?" Rae joked under her breath.

"I don't trust him," Devon said seriously, staring into Carter's eyes. "I never have, not from the moment he joined up with the Privy Council. Now, if we're going to be—"

"Hang on," Molly interrupted with a wide grin, "*that's* what this is all about? I thought you just didn't like the way he was looking at Rae."

Rae wrinkled her nose in distaste. "What way? There was no way."

"There was a way."

Julian chuckled, tracing his long fingers against the table. "That's pretty weak, Dev. You've got to stand your ground and fight—you can't just send him outside."

Devon's cheeks turned pink. "I'm not just sending him out—"

"You literally asked him to go fetch some wood."

"Beth did!" Devon said defensively. "That's not the point—"

"What *is* the point, Mr. Wardell?" Carter cut in, ending their little squabble. "Because, although I respect your judgement, we're running dangerously low on time, and I need to know what's going on."

Devon took a deep breath and squared his shoulders. "Cromfield's coming after Rae. That's his end game. Everything he does between now and then, he's doing for *that* sole purpose.

Now you say he's after a brainwashing device? A piece of which just mysteriously went missing?"

"Devon," Carter said more gently, "I completely understand your nerves, and at this point you have every right to be a bit paranoid, but Gabriel risked his life to get Rae out of prison. To imply that he had something to do with—"

"I'm not implying that," Devon said quickly. "I understand the magnitude of the risk he took, and I'm sincerely grateful. *I am.*" He shot a look at Molly and Julian, who were still grinning away. "But the fact remains: we don't know him. We don't know whose radar he unintentionally put himself on by helping Rae— we don't know the kinds of things he'd be forced to say if he was interrogated: No matter which way you cut it—the less he knows, the better; for his sake as well as ours." His eyes flicked ever so briefly to Rae before locking on Carter without compromise. "And in the end, this is Rae's safety we're talking about, and I'm not taking any chances."

There was a fierce determination in his voice that no one in the room could question. It went abruptly quiet as the light banter suddenly vanished, and the stakes they were playing with fell heavily into place.

"We don't need to involve him further," Julian finally agreed, passing his phone to Molly as she held out her hand for it. "He's already done more than enough to help. Send him back to London—he can keep an eye on things from the inside."

"And in the meantime," Molly muttered, her fingers texting at the speed of light, "I'm going to get started trying to figure out this new leak..."

"I'm sorry," Beth had stopped making sandwiches and was standing at the head of the table, a loaf of bread and a butter knife still in her hands, "I'm still stuck on the fact that I just saw a fully-coordinated teenage meltdown." She shook her head incredulously, glancing outside to where Gabriel was assumedly stacking wood. "That whole time, you were all just—"

Devon flashed an apologetic grin. "I'm afraid we're not as delicate as all that."

She and Carter exchanged an unreadable glance before Carter shook his head, bringing his fingers up to his temples. "Now you see what I have to deal with every day. *Teenagers.*"

"That hot chocolate does sound great though, Mrs. K." Julian leaned back in his chair with a charming smile.

"And the sandwiches, Mom!" Rae added. "We're starved!"

Bethany burst out laughing and walked slowly back to the counter, shaking her head as she began plopping the sliders onto plates.

There was a little *buzz*, followed by a triumphant grin as Molly handed Julian back his phone.

While none of the rest of the teenagers seemed to think this was at all strange, Carter slapped the table hard to get Molly's attention. "Circling back—what exactly were you saying, Miss Skye? You're going to get started figuring out the leak?" His voice took on a hint of condescension. "I can assure you that I have my best people already working on the issue from within the Council itself. If there's a leak there, *I'll* find it. I don't know what little scheme you had in mind, but—"

"It's not a little scheme," she bristled defensively. "I'm just getting my boyfriend in on it as well, that's all." Her face turned almost smug. "You'd be surprised what he can accomplish when he sets his mind to it..."

Rae gagged again silently, but the whole thing went right over Carter's head.

"You're passing your *boyfriend* sensitive information?" He looked at her like she just might have gone mad after all. "What on earth would make you do such a thing?!"

"Well, he's not your everyday boyfriend," Molly answered cryptically. "Let's just say he has some connections with the...um...other side."

"The other side?!"

"Oh! Oh no! No, no, no. Not Cromfield!" Molly said quickly. "Julian's the one dating someone who worked for him. I'm talking about the Xavier Knights!"

"*What?!*" Carter turned to Julian with a shout, looking about ready to explode.

Julian shot Molly a quick, "leave me out of it," before sinking inconspicuously down in his chair, trying not to be noticed.

"Anyway," Molly continued on obliviously, "one of the ways we were able to out Jennifer as a double-agent back in the day, was because my boyfriend, Luke, was able to create of timeline of when exactly information started leaking from the Privy Council and ending up on the radar of the Knights—"

"Miss Skye..." Carter breathed in through his nose and out through his mouth, trying very hard to keep his composure, "are you telling me that you were made aware of the fact that the Xavier Knights had gained access to proprietary information, and you neglected to report this?"

Molly frowned, like he had asked the dumbest question in the world. "How could I have done that? Luke would have lost his job."

Rae swooped in with a helpful, "And we *did* expose Jennifer. That's the important thing."

Carter brought his hands back to his eyes. "Heaven help us..."

"The point is," Molly continued, "I just asked him to make a similar timeline to when information started slipping through the cracks *this* time. He says it will take a while, but he'll get right on it."

"This is just perfect," Carter mumbled, staring across the table with red-rimmed eyes. "You're placing the future of this organization in the hands of your...your *flavor of the month.*"

Rae snorted into her hand as Molly flushed bright red. "He is not just a *flavor of—*"

"Why did you need my phone to text Luke, anyway?" Julian asked curiously, casually stopping her rant before it could begin.

She shrugged distractedly and pulled out her own. "It was long distance. I don't need those sorts of charges."

"So, we'll keep Gabriel at an arm's length for now," Rae summarized, "for his protection as well as our own. In the meantime, we'll focus on collecting these pieces before Cromfield can get his grubby little hands on them."

"You know," Molly mused aloud, taking a gulp of hot chocolate, "in a way, we're lucky Cromfield is only after the device. What if he was going after something else? Like a bomb?"

"That's very true," Rae nodded unblinkingly at the wall. "Or, like, a dragon. Something he resurrected from the old days to rain down fire and brimstone."

"No fire and brimstone." Molly grinned and slurped up a marshmallow. "Glass half full."

Beth's eyes narrowed as she set a stack of plates on the table. "You know, you guys might have been playing it up back there, but this job is seriously doing a number on you."

The four of them shared a blank expression before digging into their food.

Carter watched them eating for a moment, murmuring in a low voice, "I'm not even sure that going after Cromfield is the right end game anymore. If the only thing he's really after is Rae, the best thing to do might be to keep her as far away from him as possible."

Devon looked up, like he thought this was a magnificent idea, but before he could say anything Rae cut him off.

"Hey," she said through a mouthful of turkey, "if Cromfield wants to come after me, he knows right where I am. The last time we spoke on the phone, I basically told him as much."

"What?! You spoke to him on the phone?!" Beth and Carter exclaimed at the same time.

Rae paused in her chewing and looked across the table at Molly. "I thought you guys told them all that already."

"No, I totally forgot about that part," Molly answered, taking another gulp of chocolate. "In fact, I can't even remember when exactly that happened. Was that in Japan? Or after we fought Angel and helped her fake her own—" Julian kicked her sharply under the table and she jerked back with a painful, "*OW!* You have *got* to stop doing that to me all the time."

"That's for telling Carter I was dating Angel." But his smirk froze on his face as a strong hand clapped down ominously on his shoulder.

"A fact that I promise you, we'll address in good time," Carter vowed in a low voice.

Julian paled and sank down again in his chair. "Yes, sir."

"*So anyway,*" Devon circled them back to the matter at hand, "the brainwashing device. Julian and I scattered three pieces. One in London, one in Ireland, and one in Wales. Now, which one did Cromfield already get?"

"The one in Wales," Carter answered gravely.

"So why doesn't the Privy Council just send people out to recover the rest of them before they can get snatched?" Rae asked impatiently.

"Because the Privy Council doesn't know any of them have gone missing, let alone who it was who took them," Carter replied. "At this rate, they'd probably think it was you; out to finish off your father's work."

"Oh, well that's just great," Rae snapped.

Cromfield did something, and she took the blame. She'd finally graduated Guilder Academy just to become a freaking scapegoat.

"We don't need the Privy Council to recover the pieces," Devon said softly, reassuringly squeezing her hand. "It's something we can do ourselves."

Her jaw tightened and she shook her head. "But we shouldn't have to..."

"Come on," his eyes sparkled as he tilted her chin up to look him in the eyes, "it'll be fun... a little road-trip to Ireland? Travelling around Britain? It's like a vacation."

"Didn't we just get *back* from vacation?" Molly muttered petulantly.

Devon flashed a coaxing smile. "Think of all the cold-weather travelling clothes Rae can conjure for us. All the, um...hats and scarves and stuff. And shoes. You like shoes, right?"

For a moment, Molly pursed her lips. Then she patted him lightly on the head. "Oh Dev, you always know exactly what to say to make me feel better."

"Gabriel's on his way back," Julian said lightly, his eyes going momentarily white before switching back to their dark brown.

Carter and Beth had been listening with amused little smiles as they bantered, but shared an abruptly-exasperated look as they glanced outside.

"Honestly, children," Beth chided, "the boy has done nothing but help."

Julian grinned. "Yeah, but beneath all this 'limit the circle of information to protect Rae' bit, the truth is that my buddy Devon's got a fragile little ego. Probably best to go along with it, for now."

Devon threw up his hands in frustration. "For the last time, that is *not* what this is about."

"Sure, sure," Molly giggled.

"Like you wouldn't punch me in the face if *I* looked at Rae like that?" Julian teased, with a playful shove. "As I recall...you actually *did* try to punch me in the face once for Rae."

"Yeah, only because you'd secretly filled your room with drawings of her! Did you draw any naked ones too? Maybe keep those ones in a secret file while you handed the rest to the Privy Council?"

Rae's cheeks steamed red and she raised her hand in the air. "A little awkward, guys. I'm right here. So's my mom! Just sitting right—"

"That was the Cromfield connection," Julian continued like she hadn't even spoken. "It was about him, not Rae. And how dare you bring that up right now! I don't know if you remember Japan, but it's still a bit of a sensitive subject." He flashed a mock look of hurt, and Molly was quick to pick up on the game.

"Geez, Dev." She rubbed Julian's back comfortingly. "Even *I* wouldn't have mentioned that. I think we all remember how badly Julian screwed everything up in Osaka. You need to be delicate—"

"Shut up!" Julian laughed, pushing her arm away.

"Were we like this at their age?" Beth muttered incredulously to Carter. "Is this really how we pumped ourselves up for a big mission?"

For the first time, Carter actually smiled. "We were worse. A lot worse."

"Guys, he's coming!" Rae interjected, her ears attuned to a pair of snow-damped footfalls outside.

The next second, Gabriel pushed open the door.

Carter and Beth shared a quick, nervous glance, but by the time they turned to the table, the four teenagers were deflated once more, back in their original poses of despair.

"Thanks for the hot chocolate, Mrs. K," Molly mumbled pitifully, sliding her hands up into her hair. "Sorry, I guess I'm just not really feeling like myself today..."

"You've got to be kidding me," Gabriel exclaimed rudely. "This is still happening?"

"I don't know what's the matter with us." Rae lifted her head an inch off the table and shot Devon a secret wink. "Maybe it's that time of the month."

"Gross!" Julian muttered. "I think we all just need some sleep."

Gabriel looked up at Carter. "See? This is why I hate working with newbies. They have no stamina." He winked at Rae. "Do you know what that is, pretty girl?"

Rae heard Devon's chair squeak as he pushed it away quickly and stood.

"She invented the word, *buddy*." Devon grabbed Rae's hand and tugged her toward the hall.

Chapter 5

"Rae?"

The sound of her mother's voice stopped her and Devon as they headed out of the kitchen. There was a catch in her mother's voice. Rae turned slowly around. "Yes?"

"Do you remember this place?"

Every head at the table swiveled from Rae to Beth then back to Rae, like a tennis match.

Rae let her eyes do a circle look, gazing out of the corner, rolling above her, to the other side and then down. "Am I supposed to?" she asked timidly, not sure if it was a trick question.

Beth smiled, her eyes shining. "This is," she cleared her throat, "this *was* your grandparents' home. I grew up here."

"Oh." She didn't know what she was supposed to say. It felt like she should feel a connection to the house, but if she did, she'd buried it long ago in childhood memories. She didn't know her grandparents, except by photos Uncle Argyle had. She wondered if the Agent 007 in the Skyfall James Bond movie felt the same kind of hollow, empty memory Rae felt now when he returned to his childhood home. Distant memories locked away somewhere. Darn, hadn't Skyfall been in Scotland too?

Her mother cleared her throat and absently tucked wisps of curls that she thought had been misplaced. "It's a big house. We still own the land and the farm around here. The fields are rented out to local farmers now, but someone kept care of the house. I think Argyle made sure it was looked after. This place belongs to you. It was left in their will to their grandchildren. It belongs to you."

"Oh." She looked around again in a kind of questioning way. What did she want with an old farmhouse in the middle of nowhere? She couldn't exactly say that to her mother. "Cool."

"Do you want me to show you around?" Beth glanced outside. "Maybe just inside the house for now. Bit cold out there to go to the barn."

"Uh, sure." Rae put on a smile and tried to look excited. This place meant something to her mother; it should mean something to her.

The farmhouse was huge, luxurious beyond what seemed reasonable in the beautiful but desolate scenery. It had five fully-furnished bedrooms upstairs, two of them with two beds each. The kitchen was stocked to the brim, and three of the four bathrooms had full, walk-in showers.

It grew dark early, and everyone agreed to an early night. They would make plans and strategize in the morning after a good night's sleep.

The problem was that there were seven people, and only five bedrooms. In what seemed like no time at all, the spacious house was filling up with everything they were all taking care not to say.

"So..." Rae began innocently, "my mom can sleep in her old room, at the far end of the house..." she paused thoughtfully for effect, "and Carter, there's a room for you right down here next to the foyer." It was her house after all: shouldn't she be in charge of the sleeping arrangements?

For what had to be one of the only times in his life, Carter turned beet red. But Beth just smiled at Rae, her eyes sparkling wickedly.

"Great, and on that note—perhaps two of the boys could share one of the remaining rooms upstairs, while you and Molly can share the other."

Rae shot her a petulant look, and Beth grinned even wider. They were square. If she couldn't be with her man, then Rae couldn't be with hers either.

"Cool, then I'll bunk with Devon."

Devon looked up in alarm while the rest of them whirled around in shock. Much to everyone's surprise, it was Gabriel who had spoken, not Julian. His green eyes sparkled with a mischievous fire as he looked his new roommate up and down, acting purposely oblivious to any tension between them.

Rae rolled her eyes at Molly and wondered if the two men would survive the night. Devon's abilities were damn-near unparalleled, but she had never seen anyone fight like Gabriel. He moved with a skill that wasn't God-given; it was developed carefully over time and backed by a casual arrogance that was just as deserved as it was annoying. Now, it seemed, he was using that same cocky self-assuredness to quietly torture her boyfriend.

"Well, I...uh..." Devon stalled, scrambling for some other solution. His eyes fell on Julian for automatic help, but before Julian could volunteer Beth clapped her hands briskly together.

"Perfect, it's settled then."

"So that just leaves you, Jules," Carter said obliviously. He gestured up the hall and to the left. "If I remember this house correctly, I believe you're up there."

Julian glanced quickly between Gabriel's triumphant expression and Devon's pained one, before a small smile crept up his face. "Brilliant—a room to myself."

For a second, his dark eyes flashed to the future. But they came almost immediately back to the present, dancing with a knowing grin. Although the specifics might be lost on everyone else, one thing was clear: this was going to be a rough night.

"Well goodnight, everyone. See you in the morning." He headed down the hall without another word. Rae suspected he was eager to escape both before Devon changed his mind, and before Carter remembered the little hiccup about him dating Angel.

"Yes, um, see you in the morning," Carter was quick to follow Julian's lead, his eyes sweeping over the children before resting briefly on Beth. "Sleep well..."

"Yes, sleep well, *headmaster*," Rae interjected, using his old school title for emphasis.

Beth swatted her upside the head and then departed to her own room, leaving the girls alone in the hallway with Devon and Gabriel.

"So...top bunk? I'll flip you for it. Or you wanna arm-wrestle?" Gabriel was looking decidedly pleased with himself, while Devon had a look on his face like he couldn't believe what had just happened to him.

He muttered a few words Rae had never heard come out of his mouth before, then he leaned down and kissed her swiftly on the lips, bidding her goodnight. As he walked away, Molly flitted behind him like a shadow, hiding her smile as the two of them disappeared up the stairs.

Which left Rae alone with the man who was turning out to be an endless thorn in her side.

"Finally," Gabriel held open his arms with a look of utter exhaustion. "Come here."

"Bite me."

One would think with four working bathrooms in the house, it would be possible to have a moment of privacy. The night, it seemed, had other plans.

"Oh, hello!" Gabriel popped up behind Rae in the doorway, scaring her half to death.

She had been standing in front of the mirror in a pair of hastily conjured pajamas, brushing her teeth. The shower situation hadn't been easy. Apparently, the country of Scotland had a limited supply of hot water, but she had managed to do the entire thing without running into Gabriel once.

Until now.

"Geez!" She jumped out of her skin, placing a hand over her heart. "What's the *matter* with you?!" Then her eyes swept over the rest of his outfit, or rather, what was left of it. "Gabriel, for the last time, put on a damn shirt!"

"I *told* you," he pretended to be as flustered as she was, intentionally pressing against her as he reached for a spare toothbrush, "I get hot in the night. You should remember that." He winked.

Her fingers crackled with electricity and he leaned back a few inches. "Careful, now," she mocked seriously. "We're not on a ship anymore. And I don't think anyone in this house would have a problem with me frying your ass."

He sniffed carelessly, observing his perfect jawline in the mirror. "Yeah, your boyfriend seems to feel the same way. Such *hostility* in this place."

Remembering the forced sleeping arrangements, Rae turned her back to the mirror to face him straight on. "Yeah, speaking of... why did you have to do that?" she hissed between her teeth, well aware that at least one other person in this house was blessed with super hearing.

Gabriel's eyebrows shot up in innocent surprise. "What? Volunteer to spend the night with your boyfriend? Well, I figured at least one of us should do it, poor guy. And since you were so publically relegated to the girls' room,' I thought—"

"Would you be serious for one second?" Rae tried to hold back her smile. The boy was infuriating. "Why would you do that to him? You know he doesn't like you."

Gabriel took a casual step forward, inadvertently trapping her between the sink and his towering, bare-chested, muscular body. As his long legs pressed up against hers, she sucked in a quick breath, wishing like hell he didn't smell like citrus body wash—

wishing he smelled like something rotten instead of hunky, delicious male.

"Yeah," he breathed, smiling down at her, "I was pretty clear on that when he faked a meltdown just to get me outside so you guys could talk without me."

Rae's breath caught in her chest, but he merely smiled.

"I'm not an idiot, Rae, although I did enjoy the performance. And you know, to be honest, I can't really blame him." He leaned down slightly, his warm breath fluttering the tips of her hair. "If you were my girlfriend, I'd be pretty damn protective of you as well."

"Fortunately, she's not."

Both Gabriel and Rae whirled around to see Devon standing framed in the doorway. He took a deliberate step forward, causing Gabriel to step back. They were approximately the same height, and stood eye to eye for a moment before Rae cleared her throat.

"I...um...I can't breathe," she muttered, sandwiched tightly in the middle.

Gabriel stepped back farther still, but Devon stood his ground, a telltale muscle in his jaw twitching as his normally-sparkling eyes grew suddenly cold. "There are at least three other bathrooms in this place," he said with no pretense or games. "Brush your damn teeth somewhere else."

Gabriel's eyes flashed for a second—up for the challenge—before he raised his hands innocently and backed away with an easy smile. "All done anyway. Nice talk, Rae. *Devon*."

Devon shut the door firmly behind him and fell back against it, gritting his teeth with what looked like only a very thin layer of self-control. "I think I might kill him."

"Dev," Rae tried to temper his rage, "you can't kill him." Was he jealous? Green because Gabriel was flirting with her, or because he was worried he might not measure up? She shook her head. *Now why would I think that? Of course Devon would measure up. Wait! He'd more than measure up. He's oodles above Gabriel.*

"Why not? People die in their sleep all the time. I'd make it look like an accident."

"Yeah, I'm not sure that would—"

"Like he choked on my fist." He held his hand up and clenched his fingers, twisting it in the air to show Rae.

She snorted in laugher, and the sound snapped Devon out of his murderous trance.

He glanced over at her, and his face softened into a lovely smile, dimple included, as he pulled her closer. "Come here." His lips lowered down to hers. "You know, I haven't even gotten to kiss you properly since you broke out of jail."

Rae stood up on her toes, her teeth tugging playfully on his bottom lip. "Does it make it more exciting for you? Now that I'm a felon?"

"I don't know. Maybe." He grinned. "Yes."

His long fingers wrapped around her thighs, and the next second, she was sitting on the counter. They grinned at each other, but stayed perfectly quiet as they came together, fingers tangling in each other's hair. Within just a few second, Rae's legs wrapped automatically around his waist—anchoring him even tighter to her as her hands began wandering down his shirt. His breathing quickened, and he had just reached up to pull it over his head, when there was a sudden pounding on the door.

"Hey, if you guys are done *snogging* in there, some of us still need to use the shower," Molly called through the door, loud enough to wake up the whole house.

Devon's eyes snapped shut and Rae bit her lip apologetically. "She's a little high-strung..." she whispered teasingly, giving him another quick kiss on the neck.

His shoulders fell with a regretful sigh before he unlocked the door. "Perfect timing as ever, Molls. It's all yours."

Molly bustled into the room with a bag of toiletries bigger than Rae's whole suitcase. She completely ignored the two of them as she started placing various bottles in alphabetical order on the counter, only pausing to nudge Rae off of it and back onto the floor. "You know," she sniffed, "the two of you could be a little more sensitive. Not all of us are as lucky enough to have our significant others here like you...and your mom," she added with a grin.

"Ugh—stop!" Rae flicked over a bottle on purpose. "You're as bad as Gabriel."

Molly's eyes flashed. "*No one* is as bad as Gabriel! Did you know that as I was walking in here, he asked me if I wanted company in the shower?" She shook her head in disgust. "The boy may be beautiful, but he's a menace. He needs to be stopped."

"Like he choked on his own shoe..." Devon murmured, his eyes far away.

"What?"

"Ignore him," Rae said pointedly, shoving him out the door. "Goodnight, babe; try not to kill anyone before breakfast."

He backed down the hall with a wicked grin. "I can't be held responsible for what may or may not go down in that room. Accidents happen all the time..."

She shut the door with a smile and turned back to Molly in exasperation. "I know it sucks that Luke's not here, but honestly, sometimes I think you guys are the lucky ones. At least you never find yourselves in situations like this."

"Trapped in your mother's old house with two hot guys trying to get up your skirt?"

"Molly Skye!"

"What?" she giggled, and dodged the hand-towel Rae threw at her. "At least you've had some actual face-time with your boyfriend. Sometimes it feels like Luke and I are living through a phone."

Rae paused, a little thrown off-balance by the abruptly thoughtful words. "I guess it is kind of a long-distance relationship right now, huh?"

Molly pursed her lips and nodded, sorting continuously through her things.

"And is Luke..." Rae continued cautiously. "Is he okay with that?"

The last bottle fell into place and Molly turned with a small sigh. "He knows we'll have a future soon. A normal life, with normal activities, and... relatively normal jobs in London. I mean, that's what we're going through all of this for, right?" She gestured around. "To have a future?"

"Yeah," Rae answered quietly, "I guess you're right."

But as she went to bed that night, she couldn't be so sure. She'd just been broken out of jail and smuggled out of the country on a fishing boat. And that was by no means the strangest thing that had happened to her lately.

Was there ever going to be 'normal' for her and Devon? At this point, was it even possible?

Despite the feast weighing down the table, breakfast the next morning was a subdued affair.

Julian had stayed up late texting Angel, though he wouldn't admit it. Molly had stayed up late texting Luke, which she wouldn't shut up about. And Devon and Rae had stayed up late texting each other stuff they didn't want anyone to know about.

Gabriel, as it turned out, had left in the early hours of the morning to catch the ferry and return to London. While Devon was openly thrilled about his departure, he was slightly less than enthusiastic about the present he'd left behind for Rae: a crude, hand-drawn depiction of the two of them sleeping together on the boat.

Needless to say, the only cheerful *awake* people sitting around the table that morning were Beth and Carter.

His eyes glanced over the mountains of eggs, biscuits, and gravy with a faint smile. "Like mother, like daughter." She met his eyes and they shared a warm smile.

"What's that supposed to mean?" Rae asked loudly, intentionally breaking the moment.

Beth rolled her eyes but patted her daughter on the hand. "Not you and me, Rae. Me and *my* mother. She was...well, let's just say she was a bit of a cook."

"That's an understatement," Carter exclaimed merrily. "I only came here one time before—and actually it was under some rather grave circumstances. But even then, that woman flew around the kitchen like it was she who was inked instead of your father."

"Why did you come here?" Rae asked, genuinely curious. "What were the grave circumstances?"

Carter's face froze still as a statue, before it tightened. "I came here to tell them and your Uncle Argyle the news of your mother's death."

The table was quiet for a moment as everyone took deliberate sips of coffee, avoiding everyone else's gaze.

"So," Beth clapped her hands with forced levity, "you kids ready to go to Ireland?" She gazed at the pairs of blood-shot eyes around the table before pushing to her feet. "Maybe I'd better put on some more coffee..."

They quickly finished eating, and went about packing up their things. The unofficial plan was that, as they recovered each piece, they'd return with it to Scotland before setting out to find the next. Although it was going to mean a lot of extra travel time, everyone agreed that it would be far too dangerous to carry multiple pieces around with them when there was already a target on their backs.

It also meant that, with any luck, Rae was going to see her mother again in just a few days.

"See, sweetheart, it's not so bad," Beth assured her as they strolled around the grounds. The boys were already throwing their suitcases into the trunk, but Molly was still frantically racing through the house, trying to collect her absurd number of things. "I'd come with you in a heartbeat, but James told me that a representative of the Council is going to be coming by the day after tomorrow to 'check in on me,' make sure I'm holding up through the ordeal of my daughter's incarceration and subsequent escape." She laughed sharply. "In reality, they're just making sure that you're not hiding out here. But I'll give them the full tour. They won't find anything."

They came to a stop in the barn, the sweet smell of hay mixed with the scent of freshly cut grass carried inside by a gentle breeze.

"It's amazing in here..." Rae stared around in wonder, sitting absentmindedly on a bench pushed up against the corner. "I still can't believe this is where you grew up."

Beth gave her a strange look for a moment, before sitting beside her. "It's more than where I grew up," she said quietly. "It's where I met your father."

Rae looked up with a start and Beth offered her a sad smile.

"He came back for the winter holidays with your uncle one year. They were best friends at school." A dark shadow passed over her face as she ran her hands along the smooth wood. "This was always my spot, you know? I'd sneak out here all the time to get away from the house, from my family. It was the only place I could really just relax and think." Her eyes took on a faraway look as she gazed up through the open window. "It's where your father and I fell in love. I'd read to him for hours on this little bench. It's actually where we had our first kiss..."

Rae couldn't think of anything to say. She just stared down at the worn wood, a tangle of emotions running through her head.

So this was it, huh? Where all the magic started?

And what if it hadn't?

What if Simon Kerrigan had never married Beth? Rae would never have been born, of course, but maybe a lot of other things wouldn't have happened either.

Maybe he would never have spun so far off the deep end, or if he still did—maybe it would have been spotted sooner and a lot of innocent people wouldn't have lost their lives. Maybe he would have ended up with Kraigan's mother instead? Or even Jennifer? Maybe he would have spent his life alone.

One thing was for certain: if it hadn't been for that magical holiday and this little bench, Rae wouldn't be about fly to Ireland to search for a missing brainwashing device.

The car honked from the drive, and both Beth and Rae hid their emotions in time to share a brief smile. As they walked out into the sun, Beth pulled Rae in for a huge hug, whispering, "You be safe now, you hear me? You come back to me in one piece."

Rae grinned. "I always do, Mom. They've yet to get a piece of me."

They chuckled softly, but as Rae pulled away her eyes flicked again to the barn. As much as she'd initially loved it, there was something about the place that was deeply disturbing. Something she couldn't quite place. Something that wedged itself deep in the back of her mind.

Chapter 6

Dear Rae,

I had to leave before dawn to catch the ferry, but I wanted to wish you good luck. I'm afraid with Cromfield after you, you're going to need it. Just keep your head down and be careful. Don't go sticking your neck out for no reason. It's such a pretty neck. I wouldn't want anything happening to it...

Take care of yourself,

Gabriel

xx

P.S. I hope Devon likes my picture.

Rae mentally cringed as she crumpled the note into a little ball, remembering full well the look on Devon's face when he saw the hand-drawn picture of her and Gabriel sleeping together on the fishing boat. *That* had taken some explaining. She'd found this note under her pillow that morning. Yes, *under* it. How Gabriel had managed to put it there? She had no earthly idea.

"Rae? You coming?"

Rae lifted her head to see Julian, Molly, and Devon all waiting for her in the aisle of the plane. They had landed at Shannon Airport on the western coast of Ireland a few minutes ago, and were off to the lower terminal to rent a car.

She quickly stuffed the note into her pocket and snatched up her carry-on bag as she shimmied out between the seats. Then, almost as an afterthought, she pulled the crumpled paper back out of her jacket and tossed it on the empty chair.

Why would she keep it? For Devon to find *again*?

Molly shot her a strange look, but said nothing as the four of them hurried off the plane and down to the lower levels of the airport. They had checked no luggage. In fact, they'd come to the group realization that they wouldn't have to be checking luggage any longer. Rae could conjure them whatever clothes they needed, as well as a suitcase to put them in. Sometimes, being a superhero had its advantages. Why get stuck at the baggage claim?

"So are you going to tell me what that note said?" Molly whispered as she and Rae slid into the backseat of the spacious SUV.

Rae pinched her hard in the side as her eyes darted up to where Devon and Julian were filling out the last of the insurance paperwork. "How many times do I have to tell you?!"

"Your boyfriend has super-human hearing, yeah, yeah, I know..." Molly grinned. "You'll have to tell me later, though." Then, without another word, she scrambled out of her seat and settled in the passenger's seat just as Julian was opening the same door.

He took one look at her, pursed his lips, then decided to pick his battles. Shaking his head slowly, he closed the door again and settled in the back with Rae.

"Don't take it personally," Rae clapped him on the shoulder good-naturedly. "I think she wants to be navigator."

"Again?" He glanced at the back of Devon's head. "This should be good."

As the car revved to life, Molly began noisily unfolding a map that was bigger than she was, unintentionally poking Devon in the side of the head. He knocked it away with a slightly irritated expression and met Julian's eyes in the rear-view mirror.

"I thought you were sitting up here with me," he said softy.

"Nope! No Julian. I decided to help us with the route," Molly replied cheerfully. "After all, we wouldn't want to have another Bakersfield incident, would we?"

Rae and Julian stifled their smiles as Devon threw up his hands. "For the last time, that was *planned*. I was trying to waste some time because Julian said the station wasn't going to open up for another forty minutes."

"Then there was that time in Poland..."

"Out of the car!"

Rae discreetly kicked the back of her friend's seat as her boyfriend's blood pressure shot through the roof.

"Alright, alright," the tiny brunette conceded, flipping the map the right side up. "There's no harm in asking for directions, that's all. But that's the *last* thing I'm saying," she added quickly when everyone in the car shot her a look or kicked her seat.

It went quiet for a bit as they pulled out onto the interstate; a few precious minutes that everyone knew were too good to last...

"Are you sure you know where you're going?"

Devon closed his eyes painfully. "*Yes*, Molly Elizabeth. *Yes*."

She held up her hands. "No need to get defensive. I'm just making sure."

Julian and Rae shared another look in the backseat, both making efforts to stop their laughter from escaping.

"Well, I'm sure. I have a damn fennec fox tatù! My sense of direction is good!" Devon snapped as they shot down the freeway. "You know, sometimes you make me really glad that I never had a sister."

"I know!" Molly exclaimed, misinterpreting entirely. "Could you imagine? Between her and Rae and Julian, when would *we* ever get to spend quality time together?"

Devon shot her a long, hard look. "You're joking, right?"

Julian stared out the window with a smile. "And...we're back."

"Yep," Rae grinned, "the road-trip is officially underway."

They made it to a tiny town called Doolin just as the sun was setting over the horizon. Carter had called ahead and made reservations in a gorgeous quaint hotel designed to look like a medieval castle. It was set just a few blocks away from the rocky cliffs, surrounded by rolling fields of emerald green, and had a stunning view of the sparkling ocean.

"*This* is the way to travel," Rae said appreciatively as they walked inside and set down their bags. While the entire town was incredibly rustic—Molly had accidently tripped over what turned out to be an actual sheep on the way in—the little hotel had a fully-stocked fridge and was decked out with all the newest appliances.

"It's also got Carter's fingerprints all over it," Devon said quietly, coming up behind her and circling his arms around her waist with a smile. "Two beds."

Rae whirled around, still pressed up against him. "What?"

"It's a shared suite, so we're all together, but there's just one bed in both of the rooms." He grinned. "I guess they're kind of counting on the fact that Julian and Molly won't share a bed no matter how much we ask them, so you and I will stay separated."

"*They?*"

He grinned again. "When I said that this has Carter written all over it, I meant Carter and your mom."

Rae shook her head, grimacing, just as Molly came bounding up out from a room behind the kitchen. "Rae, this is so great! We're roomies again! Just like at Guilder..." A nostalgic look crossed over her face and she skipped back the way she came to start unpacking.

"Get dressed, Molly; we're going out tonight," Julian instructed as he came out of the opposite room, looking incredibly, effortlessly handsome in a suit. He tossed Devon a brochure he'd been reading, then settled on the couch to wait beside Rae.

"Well...hello there, 007," she said approvingly.

He grinned, stretching his arms out in front of him. "You did an awesome job with the suit, Rae. Honesty, this is better than my tailor."

She let out a bark of laughter. "You have a tailor? What is this, 1925?"

A faint pink tinted the tops of his cheekbones and he shoved her playfully to the side. "It's not *my* tailor. It's the Privy Council's. He decks us out sometimes, for certain kinds of missions."

"Yeah, sure," she teased as Devon walked over, waving the brochure in the air.

"This is perfect," he said, eyes locking on Julian.

Julian shrugged. "I know. And it's going to work, too. It's almost like..." his face grew absurdly serious, "it's almost like I can see the future..."

Rae laughed again, snatching the brochure out of Devon's hand. "*What* is so perfect?" Her eyes clouded over the longer she read. Eventually, she looked up with a very doubtful expression on her face. "A match-making festival? Is this even real? They have these?"

"They have them," both boys answered in unison, before glancing in opposite directions.

"It's the perfect opportunity for us to get the piece," Devon continued. "It's kind of in a...a tricky place to get to. Especially without being seen. But this will be perfect. The town only has a few hundred people, and this is a huge annual event. Everyone will be there."

Rae was unconvinced. "And what if Cromfield or one of his little minions is out there right now, stealing it as we speak? I really think we should just get it over with and—"

"They can't get to it now," Devon assured her quickly. "And neither can we. It's protected."

Her face screwed up. "By what?"

Devon and Julian shared a superior look.

Her boyfriend shot her a cocky grin. "By the tide..."

"I don't know. I'm thinking I should've gone with the green..."

Rae rolled her eyes, combing out her hair and letting her dark tresses spill in little waves down her back. "We're not really participating in the festival, you know that, right, Molls? We're just killing some time there and making sure we weren't followed until the peak of low tide when we can get the missing piece."

Molly made a face, pinning her hair atop her head in an elegant knot. "Yeah, I know. But that doesn't mean we can't look *stunning* doing it. I mean, we want to fit in, right?"

"Yeah, we want to fit in, but—"

Molly skipped over to stand next to her in the mirror, giving both of them a satisfied nod. "Well, mission accomplished!"

Rae couldn't help but grin. The way her friend started legitimately hyperventilating over fashion would never cease to amaze her. And she had to admit, they looked pretty damn good.

Molly, for all her girlish eccentricities, looked like a fairytale princess. Like the little mermaid come to life. She was wearing a long gown of blinding white silk, with a low-cut neckline accentuated by a diamond brooch. Her flaming hair stood in stark contrast to both the dress and her pale skin, making her bright green eyes and rosy red lips seem to pop right off her face.

Rae had gone a different direction.

"You look like one of those sirens," Molly said appreciatively, smoothing down the fabric with delicate fingers. "You know, one of those mythological creatures that so were beautiful they lured men to their deaths?"

Rae gave her a rather startled expression, and she laughed.

"Trust me, that's a good thing."

"Ladies, the festival's already started," Devon called from the living room.

Molly raised her chin like royalty and shot Rae a gleeful grin. "Shall we?"

It would be impossible to accurately describe the look on the boys' faces when Rae and Molly appeared on the landing.

It didn't matter that they were grown men, it didn't matter that they were international super-agents, it didn't matter that they happened to look like Greek gods themselves.

In that moment, they were just teenage boys again.

There was a flurry of throat clearing and needless tie-straightening as Julian made a conscious effort to look the other way.

Devon, on the other hand, made a beeline right for Rae. "You...are..." He simply trailed off, eyes wide as they swept shamelessly over her body. "I changed my mind," he said a little louder, glancing at the others. "No festival. You and Molly can get the piece. Rae and I will...guard the hotel room."

Molly gigged aloud as Rae flashed him a bewitching grin, swirling the folds of her red gown beside her. While Molly had gone with a wintery-white, Rae had conjured a dress that looked like pure fire. The blood-red silk clung to her thin body before cascading down to the floor, offset by an onyx and ruby necklace. Her makeup was minimal, save for a smoky eye, and her hair fell free in loose waves. But the power of the dress was undeniable.

'Fire and Ice,' she and Molly had jokingly called it. They aimed to make a splash in this little town, and they were going to do it tonight.

"Very funny, lover boy, but we're on a *mission* here," Molly teased in an uncharacteristic bout of professionalism. "We've got to get going." She glanced beside her to where Julian was still looking deliberately the other way. "Jules—"

"I love Angel," he blurted. Something he'd clearly been chanting to himself.

Molly and Rae shared a quick, smug look, while Devon clapped his friend sympathetically on the shoulder. "Are you sure you won't bunk with Molly so I can sleep with Rae?" he muttered with a playful smirk, seeing the look on Julian's face. "Just for one night?"

"That's cold, man. Really cold." Julian pulled himself together with a grin. "And no, I won't." Then Rae swept towards them and his eyes widened. "But I will sleep on the couch, because, you know... Far be it from me to stop you from—"

"Hey," Rae said brightly, tossing back her hair, "you guys ready to go?"

They fell speechless once more and she rolled her eyes.

"Come on, you two," she grabbed their hands and pulled them forward, "let's get on with it..."

The match-making festival was being held in a rustic old pub from the 1500s, and, judging from the number of people flooding the streets, almost the entire town had to be there.

Traditional Irish folk music blared from inside, played by a band who was drinking more than everyone in the first row of the audience combined, and as Rae stretched up on her toes to see past the line inside, she felt a shiver of excitement run up her spine.

Mission or no mission, they were at least here right now. And she couldn't remember the last time the four of them had a chance to really let loose like this.

They *had* missed all the graduation parties. They *did* deserve a little breather. Why not take advantage? They were already dressed for the part.

Indeed, the four of them were attracting far more than their share of looks as they finally edged up in line to stand in front of the bouncer. The man was easily nine-feet tall, Rae thought in wonder, as she tilted her head upwards to get a better look at his face.

His eyes swept appreciatively over the girls, but stopped cold on the boys. They narrowed with the faintest trace of jealously and dislike, and his mouth thinned to a hard line.

Apparently, he didn't want the competition.

"No couples," he said harshly, folding his arms across his chest. "This is a place to find matches. You don't come already in pairs."

"No, no," Devon said quickly, trying to make amends, "these are my...cousins."

The man raised his bushy eyebrows in blatant disbelief. "Your cousins?"

Rae had to admit it wasn't Devon's best story. Standing there, framed in the glowing sunset, the four of them couldn't look more different.

Molly was clearly from a place like this, dark auburn hair and alabaster skin, while Rae's long raven locks tumbled down past startlingly blue eyes. While they were both thin, they stood at vastly different heights, and no matter how hard each one tried, one spoke with a faint Scottish accent, while one had clearly spent some time living in America.

The boys were no better. While Devon and Julian were both undeniably handsome, the physical similarities stopped there. They were colored completely differently, one looking like some sort of eighteenth-century poet, and one looking like he stepped off the pages of a magazine modeling underwear for Calvin Klein.

"Your cousins," the man said again, clearly not buying their story.

"We come from a home riddled with divorce and past marriages..." Julian volunteered helpfully, before falling silent at the look on the giant's face.

Rae was certain they were about to be sent straight back to the hotel, when Molly suddenly stepped forward, pulling a tub of lipstick absentmindedly from her bag. She slowly uncapped the ruby color and spread it deliberately across her lips, seemingly oblivious to the fact that she was holding every man's undivided attention.

"Tell me," she asked in a purr, "are you allowed into the festival yourself?" She put the lipstick away and batted her eyelashes innocently at the bouncer. "When you're off duty, I mean. Will my cousin and I see you in there?" She looped her arm through Rae's, and both girls offered up a radiant smile.

The velvet rope parted, and the next moment they were inside.

"And *that's* why I've always said that girls make better super-spies than boys," Molly insisted enthusiastically, standing up on her toes to see her way to the bar.

Devon shook his head with a grin. "Yeah? Say 'super-spies' louder, will you?" But he handed her some cash and gave her an affectionate kiss on the cheek before she vanished into the crowd.

At least seven or eight guys immediately picked up on her trail, and he and Julian shared a worried glance. "I'm going to go with her," Julian murmured, locking his eyes on her flaming hair as he started to follow, "make sure everything's okay..."

"I don't know why you guys bother," Rae said with smile. "Between Julian's ink and Molly's tendency to shock first, ask questions later, I think she'll be fine."

"Old habit," Devon grinned, pulling her tight against his chest as they started to sway back and forth to the music. A pair of violins struck up an old, wistful tune, and she nestled her head contentedly beneath his chin, moving her hips in time to his steady heartbeat.

One song ended, then another. Then another.

Molly and Julian looked to be having the time of their lives, joking around together at the bar; and one by one, the rest of the crowded room was slowly dividing off into pairs.

"You know...this might not be the best idea," Rae finally said, glancing up with an impish smile. "I'm pretty sure this isn't the way you're supposed to dance with your cousin."

Devon laughed aloud and squeezed her tighter, his lips softly grazing the top of her hair.

"Maybe we're those special cousins—the ones no one ever talks about. He doesn't know..." Rae's shoulders shook with giggles. "I think he could probably squash you like a bug," she teased. "The man's a giant!"

Devon shuddered theatrically and spun her around. "I know. Stay close."

"Oh, Mr. Wardell, I intend to stay close," she breathed, staring up into his eyes.

A million different colors flashed across his face from the stage, and for a moment it seemed like it was just the two of them alone in the world. They were just a boy and a girl dancing at a bar. The sky wasn't falling, the world wasn't ending. For one of the first times in recent memory, things seemed almost normal.

"Rae..." his breath caught in his chest as the music gradually swelled, "I need to—" Then he glanced at something over her shoulder and his body went rigid. She spun around in alarm to see Julian and Molly standing at the edge of the dance floor. Julian discreetly tapped his wrist and Devon pulled away with a sigh, grabbing her wrist and leading her through the crowd.

"What?" she pressed causally, as they swept out into the cold night air, "What were you going to say?"

His eyes flickered down to hers for a split second, before he hastily looked out towards the sea. "I was going to say...that it's time to go."

Her heart fell and she fell back a step, linking arms with Molly instead.

Of course it was. Why hadn't she thought to use Julian's tatù when he first started? She might have caught what he was going to say. *But that would be spying.*

In only a few minutes, the four friends had left the town behind and were coming up on the ocean. The girls trailed behind as the boys marched up ahead.

"You know, sometimes Devon's so freaking frustrating," Rae whispered to Molly with a scarcely concealed sigh.

"Careful," Molly whispered back, hiccupping with every other step. "What's that thing you're always telling me? Your boyfriend has super-human hearing?"

Rae rolled her eyes. "He's talking to Julian, so he's distracted. But I'm serious, Molls, ever since we got together, it's like pulling teeth to get him to say what he really feels. What he's really thinking? Do you remember how long it took for us to get together in the first place? And then he broke up with me without saying a freaking word."

Molly nodded solemnly, trying to walk in a straight line. "He's a man of few words."

"No, he's not," Rae corrected distractedly. "But he lapses now and again. I know it's harping on a little point; I mean, for the most part, everything's great. And I mean, really great. Absolutely perfect. But it's just...this is our life, you know? Going to match-making events. Breaking into churches. Jetting around the world. Sometimes I wonder if we'll ever do anything normal. Will we ever *be* anything normal? And then there are moments like just now, moments where he..." she paused, "Molly? Are you drunk?"

Molly flashed an innocent smile, before hiccupping some more. "I'm sorry—what?"

Rae chuckled. "Some help you are. I need a new best friend."

"Hey," Molly tucked a loose strand of hair back into place, "Julian assured me that it was fine to drink tonight. He said the only one doing any work to get the piece will be you."

"Oh, is that right?" Rae asked indignantly, raising her voice to catch the attention of the other two. "And what exactly will *only I* be doing to recover this—"

She and Molly jumped back with a gasp as a giant wave of water exploded in the air right in front of them. It was then that she finally took a moment to look around.

The four of them had wandered far off the beaten path, making their way carefully across the uneven rocks that led out to the sea. But they were still about twenty feet above the water, and still quite a ways from the edge of the cliff, so Rae couldn't understand how she'd just gotten wet.

That's when she saw it.

"Oh...no, no, no."

She peered down into a jagged-looking crevice that stretched narrowly open in the rock before her feet. The light of the moon was only able to penetrate a few feet down, but she had a sinking feeling that the chasm stretched all the way down to the sea. Sure enough, there was another thundering crash from below, and a second later a salty spray hit both her and Molly in the face.

"Let me guess." She looked up with a glare, wiping drips of mascara from her cheeks. "All this beautiful, endless countryside, and you two geniuses hid the piece in the scary underwater cave?"

Devon looked down at his shoes, but Julian was actually quite excited. "Rae, don't you see, it's actually a brilliant spot for it! This place is hidden and completely inaccessible for all but two minutes of every day. Plus, it's almost impossible to get down there without getting ripped to shreds." His enthusiasm faded slightly as Rae's eyes narrowed. "Not that...not that *you're* going to have that problem. I'm sure you're going to be...uh...just fine."

"You don't have to do a thing," Devon reassured her quickly, taking off his suit jacket and tossing it to the side. "I can get it just fine."

Julian frowned. "Dev, you almost impaled yourself trying to get it down there to begin with—"

"What?!" Rae exploded.

"Not helping, Jules."

"You almost impaled yourself?" Rae asked directly, jabbing a finger in her boyfriend's chest.

Molly hiccupped and started to discreetly back away.

Devon raised his hands soothingly. "Only a little, babe. You know Julian; prone to exaggeration, that one."

"No. Not really," Rae countered. Then she looked down into the ominous chasm with a sigh. "How much time do we have?"

Julian glanced at his watch. "The tide's going to be at its lowest point in about a minute. Once it is, you'll have another sixty seconds to lower yourself down and get the piece."

Rae nodded, rubbing her hands together like an Olympic diver about to take a leap. "And what does this piece look like?"

Julian bit back a smile. "Hon, it's going to be the only thing in there that isn't rock and looks like a brainwashing device."

"Right. Got it."

"Hang on a second," Devon pulled her back. "You are absolutely not going down there. It was always going to be me who did it. That was the plan!"

"It was a bad plan," Julian murmured as Rae said, "Yeah, that's a terrible freaking plan."

"You got this, Rae," Molly chimed in from the grass several yards away. "Just don't mess it up. And do you think you could conjure me a blanket before you go? It's really cold out here."

Rae shot her a look as Julian began counting down the seconds on his watch. "Yeah, you're not the one about to jump into the ocean, Molls. You can live with it for another sixty seconds."

"...nineteen, eighteen, seventeen..."

"Whatever you do, don't just jump in," Devon warned, finally accepting that he was outnumbered and shifting his focus instead to help. "It's not a straight shot down; the rocks stick out from every angle. They'll rip you up if you jump."

"Then what do you suggest?" Rae exclaimed, feeling nervous for the first time.

"...twelve, eleven, ten, nine, eight..."

"Make a rope and we'll lower you down," Devon said quickly. "You'll find the piece no problem once you're there. The only trick is to pull you back up before the time runs out, or..."

"...or what?" Her mind ran through a hundred scenarios, all of them ending terribly. She couldn't die, but what if she was paralyzed because of a jagged rock slicing her back? What if she lost feeling and couldn't control her tatùs? She swallowed hard.

"Don't worry. We'll pull you back up in time."

"OR WHAT?!"

"Rae," Julian interjected, "go now!"

Before she had time to think about it, a rope was in her hands. She looped one end quickly around her waist, while the boys took the other. Then, with a silent prayer, she was lowered down into the darkness as fast as she could.

If the chill on the surface was getting hard to take, it was nothing compared to what it was like in the little cave. Rae started shivering uncontrollably as she held up a hand with her mother's fire, illuminating the jagged, black rocks on every side. The night sky seemed very far away now the lower she went, and after only a few seconds she heard a loud tear.

"You know," she shouted up, "you could have warned me about what we were going to do before I put on this ridiculous dress!"

One of the boys shouted something back, but she was unable to hear it over the deafening rush of the foaming sea. A briny smell of salt and rust filled her nostrils, and she coughed loudly before tugging suddenly on the rope as her toes dipped down into the water.

"I'm down!" she called, raising the light in her hand quickly to look around the claustrophobic cave.

Well this is just...perfect.

There was no device. There was no fragment or shard of it. There was quite simply, nothing down there but rock.

"Guys!" she screamed to make herself heard over the swelling tide. "It's not here!"

They might have shouted something back, but it was lost over the steady crescendo pouring in from just beyond the cliffs.

Okay, think, Rae. Think.

By her estimation, she only had about ten seconds left. If she was going to get this piece and get back up before she was dashed to smithereens against the rocks, she'd have to do something *now*!

But just then, as she was beginning to lose herself to hypothermic panic, the strangest thing happened. There was a subtle shift deep inside her body, and something warm buzzed to the surface of her skin. She took a second to recognize it, before closing her eyes in relief.

"Of course..." she breathed.

If Gabriel could manipulate metal, then he could surely sense metal as well.

She lifted out her hand, scanning blindly in the dark, only to find the piece very quickly. It had apparently fallen from its original perch, lodging itself several feet below the rising tide, but it flew up into her hand as if she'd called for it by name.

The next second, the water began to overtake her.

She opened her mouth to scream, but an icy wave caught her in the face, pouring down her throat and freezing her insides. The rope went temporarily loose in her hand as she tried to keep her body from locking down in shock.

"Get me—" she spluttered and choked. "Pull me—" Another wave caught her and dragged her momentarily down before slamming her into the shards of rock. The taste of blood filled her mouth as she tilted her head back to the sky and full-out screamed. "DEVON!" She had no idea if she'd done it in her head or actually screamed. It didn't matter; she didn't have time to think.

The next second, she was flying into the air, straight back up the way she'd come.

Clutching the precious piece of metal tight in her shaking hand.

Chapter 7

"You...flew."

Rae was dripping a small pool of salt water onto the hotel room carpet, as Devon sat across from her, dripping a small pool of blood.

"I didn't actually...uh...fly, per se." He grimaced painfully as Molly did her best to pop his shoulder back into place. "But you got the piece. That's the part we should be focusing on."

Rae blinked. "No! I'd like to focus on the other part for a second, if that's okay." She cleared her throat and started again. "You *flew*."

"I told you, it wasn't—*shit*, Molly! Just do it already!"

"I can't," she grimaced apologetically, "I'm not strong enough to pull it all the way. Jules, can you?"

"Yeah." He lifted himself off the couch and crossed the room, laying his hands skillfully on his friend and popping his shoulder back into place in one swift motion.

"*Son of a—*" Devon's eyes snapped shut as he swore at the ceiling, but when he opened them again he was able to manage a smile. "Thanks," he panted in pain and relief, twisting it tentatively in front of him to test its range of motion. "Now if I could just get some antiseptic—"

"YOU FLEW, DEVON!"

Finally incensed, he threw up his hands.

"Of course I flew! You were about to get crushed and the rope was broken. What was I supposed to do?!"

"So you jumped off a cliff?!" Rae didn't know exactly why she was angry or why they were yelling, but aside from her nearly drowning, something of great significance had happened here and she was lost, trying to make sense of it.

"Of course I jumped off a cliff! *To get to you!*"

"Just hoping that you could fly us both out without KILLING yourself in the process!" She could eternally survive such physical battery. In fact, her wounds had already healed.

His had not.

"Well, actually, I—" He cut himself off suddenly, looking almost guilty. His face flushed a pale pink, surprising, considering how much blood he'd lost, and he dropped his gaze to the floor.

Rae's eyes widened in disbelief. "You didn't know that would happen. Did you?"

He glanced up for a second, before slowly shaking his head.

Her heart clenched ice cold in her chest. "You jumped off a cliff without knowing what would happen to you? Thinking you would just fall?"

"I thought I could catch you first," he murmured, "shield you from it. Then I guess...I guess my body just did what it had to do to save you."

For a moment, everyone was quiet.

Molly swooned in the background as Julian's eyebrows shot to the ceiling. "That's one way to progress your powers," he said quietly. "Life or death adrenaline."

Rae just stared silently, her blue eyes wide with tears.

"In all fairness," Devon tried to shift everyone's attention away, "I don't think I actually flew. I think it was more like I was able to jump really, really high. Launch myself off the rocks."

"Oh, so it's really no big deal then," Molly joked nervously, trying to lighten the mood. Her eyes flicked anxiously to Rae, before landing on Devon's mangled chest.

His shirt had been ripped open and one side of his rib cage had been torn in bloodied strips from where he'd covered Rae with his body, letting himself get smashed into the rocks.

"Um...Rae, why don't you make Devon some of that morphine you made for Julian back in the airport? We should also probably get some rubbing alcohol—"

But Rae was stuck on a loop, staring at Devon like she'd never seen him before. "You jumped off a cliff...without knowing what would happen to you." Without another word, she rose mechanically and headed to the nearest room. Away from everyone. The second she was inside, she shut the door behind her, collapsing against it and silently hyperventilating, like she was still back in that cave.

No, they were never going to have normal lives.

They were never going to be normal.

Not even close.

About an hour later, there was a soft knock on the door. Rae looked up silently from the bed as Devon opened it and slipped inside. There were fresh bandages around his chest and the smell of antiseptic hung heavy in the air. Julian had obviously run out to the nearest hospital to pick up supplies. Rae eyed him a bit guiltily as he sat down on the edge of the mattress, rubbing her ankle.

"You okay?" he asked quietly.

She threw back her head to stop the automatic tears. "Am *I* okay? Are you kidding?" When his face blanked, she continued. "Devon, *I can't die*. You can! And you threw your body off a cliff!"

"It seemed like a good idea at the time." He grinned but his gaze was cautious.

"Don't joke! This is serious. This could not be more serious."

"And I'm taking it seriously." His eyes grew distant for a moment, reliving scenes from the past. "Rae. Even I couldn't hear much down there, but when I heard you scream my name..." He shuddered painfully at the thought. "We don't know everything about your immortality. We're going off the word of a psychopath. We don't know if there are limits, conditions. But whether or not you can die, we know you can get hurt. You could be trapped, drowned, swept out to sea." He leaned forward and laced his fingers around her hand. "You're the only thing that matters to me. My other half, my reason to breathe. You have to know that I would—that I *could* never let that happen."

"So you jumped off a cliff—"

"Yes, I jumped off a cliff. Get over it already." He slid closer with a grin. "No part of me can lose you. When are you going to get that? And despite what those beautiful eyes are screaming at me, that's not a bad thing."

"It can make you jump off a cliff..."

He took her face gently in his hands. "It can make me fly."

Julian slept on the couch that night.

Rae and Devon stayed together in the next room. Not kissing, not sleeping, not saying a word. Just lying together, entangled in each other's arms. There was lust, but this was true love. Rae knew it. *Love harder than any pain you ever felt.*

That's what Devon had done.

When the sun's first light shone across the distant hills, he kissed her gently on the forehead and got stiffly to his feet. "Come on," he said with a gentle smile, "it's time to go."

Molly and Julian were already up by the time they pulled themselves together and wandered out to the living room. After gulping down cups of hastily-conjured coffee, they climbed into the rental car and headed back to the airport, the device piece tucked safely in Rae's bag.

In only a few hours later, they were already speeding back through the Scottish countryside, on the way back to Rae's grandparents' farmhouse.

On the way back to my *house,* she mentally corrected herself. First a penthouse in the city and now a farm in the heart of Scotland? If she ever got to stop flying all over the globe for a second, those actually might be nice places to settle down.

The car slowed dramatically as all four of them squinted in disbelief at the shiny black sports car parked in the driveway. Devon, in particular, looked less than amused.

"You have got to be kidding me..."

"Rae! Rae!" Beth was out of the house before they'd even pulled to a complete stop, both Carter and Gabriel hot on her heels. "You came back so fast, honey. Did you find it that quickly?"

Rae shot a glance at Devon, who was pulling himself painfully out of the car, eyeing Gabriel up and down with obvious dislike. "Uh...yeah. In a matter of speaking."

"Nice job, Julian. Molly. Devon," Carter congratulated, shaking each one of their hands in turn. But when he got to Devon, he suddenly stopped, scanning the young man's face with years of practice and concern. "What is it?" he asked quickly. "What's wrong?"

Devon's eyes flicked almost imperceptibly to Gabriel before he muttered, "Nothing, I'm fine."

Carter gave him a look of blatant disbelief. "You're fine? Really?" He shook his hand again, pulling it towards him a bit, and Devon wasn't able to stop from gasping in pain.

"What the hell happened?!" Both Carter and Beth exclaimed at once.

Beth stopped hugging Molly and rushed over, lifting up the corner of Devon's shirt with motherly concern before he could stop her. "Honey, what's the..." Her face turned white when she saw the gashes and painful discoloration spread across his body.

Even Gabriel offered a sympathetic grimace as he leaned forward to get a look. "Devon..." she murmured, "what happened?"

"It's nothing," he said again, a little louder this time as he yanked down his shirt. "We got in and out, recovered the piece, no one was the wiser—"

"Devon jumped off a cliff," Molly interrupted, grinning proudly at her friend.

"And then he flew back out of it," Julian added, beaming with the same pride.

Beth and Carter exchanged a quick glance, before she ventured, "And why did he do that?"

Everyone fell silent for a moment, before Rae quietly cleared her throat.

"To save me," she murmured, keeping her eyes on the ground. This time, the silence stretched on even longer. She finally brought her gaze up to look at the PC crew.

Gabriel's sympathy had vanished to sullen resentment, Carter was staring at Devon with almost paternal pride—thrilled his powers were developing—and Beth?

It was hard to understand exactly what was going on behind Beth's tear-filled eyes. She looked Devon up and down for a long time, occasionally glancing at her daughter, before she finally cleared her throat and said, "You flew?"

"Oh, I am *not* listening to this conversation again," Molly said as she picked up her bags and headed inside.

Julian was quick to follow. "Yeah, I'm out. But I'll put on some coffee."

Gabriel glanced once between Rae and Devon before turning on his heel and abruptly disappearing inside behind the others, leaving the two couples standing awkwardly in his wake.

Devon's gaze flicked between both Carter and Rae, looking for help; Carter was staring intently at Beth, and Rae was still a bit misty-eyed herself, kicking her boot almost childishly against the gravel in the drive. Eventually, he had nowhere to look but her mother.

"Can we...can we just write this off as one of those crazy things kids do and—"

"You jumped off a cliff for my daughter?" Beth interrupted. Her voice sounded almost stern, and Devon stood automatically a little straighter, ignoring the stabbing pain that followed.

"Um...yes. A bit. Only a little."

Beth stared at him for another moment, before she abruptly lifted her arm, wrapping it carefully around his bruised back. "Come on inside. Let's get you cleaned up."

She brought him inside, Carter and Rae following slowly behind. Beth took Devon carefully up the stairs to help bandage his wounds.

Rae tried listening to the noises upstairs and then stopped herself by switching tatùs to give her mother and Devon privacy. If she wanted to complain about not having a normal life, then she needed to make the effort to be somewhat normal as well. She and the others were halfway through a long breakfast by the time Beth and Devon wandered back down the stairs. Both were rather subdued, but smiling. Whatever marathon talk they'd just had must have done the trick.

And on that note...

What did my mom say to you? Rae demanded, employing Maria's telepathy the second Devon sat across from her at the table. His eyes flicked up the moment he heard her voice in his head, but his lips twitched into an innocent smile and he lifted one shoulder in an inconspicuous shrug.

Oh no! You do NOT get to keep something like this from me. What did she say? What did you say? Why were you guys up there so long?

With that same little smile, he tuned her out completely, helping himself to some sausage rolls and a proper English breakfast as he started to join the table's ongoing conversation.

You can't ignore me forever, she insisted, her eyes narrowing. *I can keep this up all day. See if you can maintain another conversation with me SCREAMING IN YOUR HEAD LIKE THIS—*

"Rae, it is impolite to use telepathy at the table," he said suddenly, giving her a look of mock disapproval before turning to her mother. "Don't you agree, Beth?"

Much to Rae's horror, Beth smiled. "I do indeed. Rae, stop being nosy. Eat your breakfast. Keep your voice out of other people's heads."

Beth? He called her *Beth*?! Whatever happened upstairs, Rae was not impressed. Not one bit.

As she sullenly dug into her eggs and bacon, Molly turned to Julian with an enthusiasm made possible only by the five empty cups of coffee in front of her. "So we got the piece from Ireland; what's next? Where's the other one you guys hid?"

Julian's eyes flicked across the table to Carter before he answered in a would-be casual voice. "It's, uh, it's in London."

"London?" Her face lit up and she turned to Rae. "Well that's perfect! Maybe we can finally spend the night in that penthouse we started renting *ages* ago!"

"Yeah, it's *where* it is in London that's the problem..." Devon glanced at Carter as well.

Rae looked nervously between them. She was starting to get that sinking feeling in the pit of her stomach. The same feeling she had long ago learned not to ignore. And they were obviously not sharing the news with Gabriel. Funny how he had been so quiet since they'd returned. *Probably listening like a hawk. Planning ways to annoy Devon and make my heart sputter when he's around.*

Carter set down his mug of coffee with a sigh. "The good news is it's nowhere all of you haven't been before."

"And the bad news?" Rae asked, bracing herself for the answer.

"It's inside the Privy Council's headquarters..."

"Well that's just it, isn't it?!" Rae threw up her hands as she paced back and forth. "Game over. We might as well put me back in chains right now."

"I can help you if that happens, sweetie," Gabriel said from the comfy chair he was reclining in.

"Calm down," Carter tried to temper her. "No one's getting thrown in chains."

"Easy for you to say," she snapped. "You weren't the one *wearing* them last time."

"So it's in PC headquarters? So what?" Gabriel leaned back in his chair with an arrogant smile. "I'm surprised at you, Kerrigan. I thought you'd be up for a little challenge."

"Don't talk to her like that, you little worm," Molly interjected with a sneer. "She has more to risk by doing this than all of us, and you know that."

"Yeah," he leaned forward with a devilish smile, "but I also know that she has the most to gain. Think about it, Rae. You go there, break in, and risk everything just to rescue the piece from Cromfield? The Privy Council will be begging you to come back. In the end, they'll have no choice but to clear your name."

Rae paused in her pacing. When he said it like that...

"Which is why I'd like to formally offer you my services."

Every head in the room swiveled his way.

"I'm sorry..." Rae stammered. "You'd like to do *what*?"

"Why should you guys be the ones to have all the fun?" he teased, giving her a wink before leaning back to look at Devon. "Besides, with wonder-boy here in a virtual body cast for throwing himself off a big rock, you guys are one man down."

Perhaps it was lucky that in the blur of angry voices that followed, Rae's mother wasn't able to hear exactly which profanity it was that her daughter said. Beth got the gist, however, and held up her hand for instant silence. "That's enough!"

Everyone around the table froze, even Carter, though he looked rather surprised to be taking orders himself. "If getting this piece and keeping it safe from this man is indeed the way to clear Rae's name, then we're going to do it. Whatever it takes, no questions asked. If this means accepting Gabriel's help," her tone silenced the protests that instantly started, "then that's exactly what you lot are going to do."

"I'm fine," Devon insisted, turning painfully in his chair to Carter. "The four of us can take care of it, just like we always do. There's no need to throw a new person into the mix; it would just be an unnecessary variable." He spoke with such calm assuredness it was almost easy to forget that what he was saying didn't exactly make sense.

Carter rubbed his temples and sighed. "Devon, breaking into the Privy Council will be one of the most dangerous things the four of you have ever tried. You'll each be placing your lives in each other's hands. You and Julian have worked together. But Rae, Molly... it's all complicated and risky. Are you really going to tell me you're up for that right now?"

Before Devon could answer, he tossed him a piece of toast.

Sure enough, while Devon's hand shot up automatically to catch it, his arm jerked back in horrific pain. He fought valiantly to keep it off his face, but he wasn't fooling anyone.

"It's settled then," Carter announced. "Gabriel comes along."

Gabriel's sparkling laugh echoed around the table. "Don't worry, bro; I'll look after your girl for you."

Devon's eyes flashed as he pushed to his feet. "I'd like to see you try, you son of a—"

"Language!" Beth yelled, as Carter commanded, "Sit down!"

Rae had sunk low in her chair, wishing the ground would swallow her whole. If there was an option to walk into the PC headquarters right now by herself—she'd take it.

"Devon's going to be coming along too," Carter clarified. "This isn't going to be a simple mission, or one that you can just improvise. The headquarters of the Privy Council is one of the most fortified places on earth. There are defenses there that you kids couldn't dream of. It's going to take a lot of planning, hard work, and a coordinated effort to get inside. And once you're there, I'd guess you have about a one in one hundred chance of getting out undetected. Devon can be the guy behind the scenes. We're going to need a bird's eye view or back entrance view. Whatever it takes."

"Except you can't help. What about Beth?"

"My mother's not joining us." Rae said in a determined voice.

"Whatever it takes?" Julian's eyes scanned worriedly to the future, but came up blank. "So, what does that mean?" he asked quietly. "If the odds are so stacked against us...?"

Carter glanced at Rae, and for the first time all morning she could have sworn she saw a hint of a smile.

She stood. "It means...we need to get to work."

Chapter 8

Rae swore she had never worked so hard in her entire life. Not at school. Not during training. Not even during finals week when she swore she'd had the worst of both worlds.

This was in a league all of its own.

"Focus, Kerrigan!" Carter shouted, "You'll need to do better than that!"

Rae rolled her eyes, but kept her comments to herself as she struggled to adjust her grip. He always called her 'Kerrigan' when they were in work-mode, she'd come to realize. 'Rae' was obviously saved for something else. Needless to say, it had been all 'Kerrigan' for the last week.

Sweat poured through her hair in little beads, falling to the ground as she clung upside-down to the outer railing of the house. She'd been hanging there for the last hour, trying to build up the strength in her upper arms. According to Carter, she was 'tiny' and 'delicate' and could use the extra muscle. Also according to Carter, she might need these skills when breaking into the headquarters of the Privy Council. When Rae had countered and asked in what part of their plan was she required to hang from the rafters like a koala, he'd sent her outside to do it some more.

"Looking good, Kerrigan." Gabriel grinned as he walked outside and squinted up at her in the sun. He tilted his head to the side, eyes sparkling as they locked on her body. "Very...flexible."

She dropped to the ground with a stifled curse.

When Gabriel called her 'Kerrigan,' it meant something else entirely. Something that set her blood boiling every time.

"And where do you think you're going?" Carter shouted angrily. "By my watch, you have ten more minutes!"

She glanced over her shoulder before throwing a dirty look Gabriel's way. He was standing casually in the frame of the kitchen door, directly blocking her path.

"I'm going inside so I don't murder our fifth wheel. Fair enough?"

"Murder?" Gabriel leaned down with a grin, bringing their faces close together. "That's a little harsh, don't you think? For the man who rescued you? And who draws you pretty pictures?"

He and the other boys had been doing their own workout in the back yard, and despite her boiling rage Rae was finding it very difficult not to look at the way his muscles gleamed in the sun.

"Pretty pictures?" she repeated shortly. "You mean of me passed out, cold, and miserable on a fishing boat? That's your big claim to fame?"

He leaned down still further and the citrusy tang of his body wash wafted into her face. "I don't remember it being so bad." He grinned again, showing her every one of his perfect teeth. "And if we're being honest," he lowered his lips to her ear, "I seem to remember we got each other heated up okay..."

"That's it!" She shoved him out of the way—hard. When he hit the bricks on the other side of the wall with a dull *thud*, she threw Carter a look of smug satisfaction. "There! Is that strong enough for you?"

Before he could answer, she disappeared inside.

Molly and Beth were standing on opposite sides of the kitchen table, staring at a pair of hand-drawn blueprints of the tunnels and hidden chambers beneath Guilder's foundations. As it was kind of an unspoken assumption that Molly wouldn't be doing much hand-to-hand combat, she and Beth had been working more on the logistical side of things. Not to say that they hadn't done their fair share of training as well.

Rae remembered that first afternoon with a smile...

Beth had taken both girls out to the middle of a huge dirt field about a mile away. Next year, it would be rented out as farm land, but for the time being it remained fallow. Rae kicked at a clump of grass and squinted around in the bright afternoon sun. Next to her, Molly was trying to keep her stiletto heels from sinking into the mud. Beth had insisted they walk here—no cars—and Rae was sure she was going to get some sort of 'Jimmy Choo needs to be treated with respect' lecture from Molly the second they were back home.

"What are we doing out here, Mrs. K?" she asked with the hint of a whine. Out of all the kids, she had the most natural relationship with Rae's mother; coming in second perhaps only to Devon, who's strange 'understanding' with Beth, Rae had yet to figure out. "And did we have to walk? I don't think there's even cell service," she added as an afterthought, lifting up her phone.

Beth chuckled to herself. "Yes, we had to walk. I'm not wasting a car on this." Both girls shot her a strange look and she chuckled again. "Alright Molly, we're going to start with you. Do you see that tree out there?"

She pointed far off into the distance, and Molly shielded her eyes as she followed along.

"Yeah, barely."

"Good. I want you to use your lightning to hit it."

Molly's eyes widened and she turned back to Beth in surprise. "Hit *that*?" She gestured with a dramatic wave of her hand. "There's no way I can hit that thing! I can barely see it. You really expect me to—"

"No, I don't expect you to hit it right away," Beth said reasonably. "But I do expect you to try. Now, let's see what you've got."

Molly groaned, lifting a dainty hand towards the tree and covering her eyes with the other. "This is going to be really embarrassing. Rae, please don't watch!"

Grinning, Rea pretended to cover her face, and peeked through her fingers as her friend shot her best bolt of lightning out across the field. It didn't even come close to the tree.

Obviously discouraged, she turned back to Beth with a 'told you so' pout, but Beth was nodding her head thoughtfully as she walked forward. "Okay, I want you to try it again. This time, square your shoulders, plant your feet, and you know that feeling you get deep in your chest when you're summoning your ink? That little sizzle? I want you to focus all your concentration on that."

"Should I spit out my gum?"

Beth stifled a sigh. "Yes, Molly. I'm going to need your full focus here."

"Got it." Molly spat it into the dirt and then did exactly as Beth asked, getting into a fixed position as she tried again. This time, the bolt went much farther, but what was perhaps more telling than the distance was Molly's reaction. Before Beth could even say anything, she opened her eyes and stared out with determination at the tree, cocking her head like she was seeing it in a whole new light. "I want to try again," she said without hesitation, assuming the position once more and squaring her shoulders. "I can do better."

Rae had never heard her sound so serious. She shot her mom a sideways smile, and Beth gave her a secret wink. Then they both turned and watched as Molly got progressively closer and closer to the tree.

Both girls went at it for the next three hours. Rae hadn't had any more luck with hitting the damn thing than Molly had, even with her fire. They were getting closer, that much was sure, but neither one had even made it a quarter of the way. After a while, Rae began to think that it was physically impossible to hit the tree. That the tree was some kind of proverbial Everest, meant only to build up confidence and control.

She and Molly had just shattered the ground with another burst of fire and lightning when they heard the sound of footsteps headed their way. They turned around to see Julian, Carter, Devon, and Gabriel walking towards them across the field. The boys were sweaty, deliciously so, from working out. Their thin tanks and dark jeans clung to their sculpted bodies in a way that made her and Molly share a quick grin before hiding their eyes from Beth.

But, as usual, there was trouble brewing in the ranks.

The second they got close enough, it was easy to see that Julian and Devon were upset about something, Carter was looking frustrated, and Gabriel looked smug. Rae stifled a sigh as she wondered what all the trouble was about this time.

Last night, it had been that Gabriel had tried to 'accidently' burst in on Rae in the shower. When Devon had moved to automatically avenge her, he'd unintentionally ripped open his bandages and the cuts beneath. By the time Rae turned off the shower, snatched up a towel, and opened the foggy door, he was bleeding through his shirt, locked in a full-on shouting match with Gabriel. The same Gabriel who had the unspeakable gall to pause mid-argument just to compliment Rae on her legs. Then Devon really lost it.

Today was shaping up to be more of the same.

"Hey guys," Beth said tentatively, sensing the same tension and trying to diffuse it before it began. "How's it going?"

Carter shot her a look like a panicked parent trapped on a field trip with a bunch of drunken kids. "It's going well. We were actually just taking a quick break—"

"*Devon* needed a break," Gabriel inserted, casting him a pitying look. "Seems someone isn't quite back to his usual self yet."

Before Devon could even reply, Julian 'accidently' shoved Gabriel face-down in the dirt. He pulled himself up and spat out a mouthful of dust, a murderous expression on his face, but before he could do a thing to retaliate, Julian lifted a finger and tapped his temple in a gesture that was as simplistic as it was absolute. The message was clear: 'Want to try something? Go ahead. I can see the future.'

Carter ignored all of them, continuing on as if he hadn't been interrupted. "We wanted to see what you ladies were up to. Maybe you can all play together for a while," he added with a strained smile.

Beth grinned. "Actually, both girls have been working really hard for quite a while now, so we were just finishing up."

"What were you trying to do out here?" Devon asked curiously, eyeing the scorched earth.

Molly put her hands on her hips, gazing out to the horizon with a determination she usually reserved for online shopping. "We were trying to hit that tree."

"*That* tree?" Gabriel took a step forward, shielding his eyes as he squinted out. "That's impossible. It's way too far away."

Rae's eyes focused on it with something akin to hunger. "Yeah...probably."

It was Carter's laughing that interrupted them. "Too far away?" He laughed again, eyes sweeping over the defeated-looking kids before landing on Beth. "They think it's too far away?"

Beth stifled a lovely smile. "They're just children, James. Let them practice."

"What?" Rae cocked her head towards her mother and put her hands on her hips. "You think you can do better?"

"The point of today was for you and Molly to practice, something at which you both excelled, and I'm very proud of you. Why don't we leave it at that?"

"Aw, come on, Mrs. K," Gabriel cajoled, with a grin, "show us your best shot. The famous Bethany Kerrigan? It's got to be something special..."

"Yeah, come on, Mom," Rae pleaded. "How close can you get?"

"How close can I get?" Beth repeated with a sparkling laugh. Her eyes flicked for a brief moment to the tree before she lifted a casual hand. "Get down."

No one moved except Carter, who crouched with a smile on the dirt. The rest of the kids just stared at her in confusion.

Eventually, Molly said, "What do you—"

"I said, *get down.*"

They had barely ducked out of the way before a wave of fire, the likes of which Rae had never seen, shot from her mother's hands in a perfect circle around the field.

The tree was gone. Only the scorched remains indicated where it had once stood. And the rest of the field? Well, it would have to remain fallow much longer.

Holy crap!! Rae pushed to her feet with her mouth hanging wide open, looking at her mother like she'd never seen her before. The other kids were in similar states of shock, though Carter was just smiling to himself, beaming at Beth with a quiet kind of pride.

As for Beth, she never gave the tree a second look. Instead, she offered a hand to Molly, who was still crouching on the ground in utter amazement.

"Shall we get back to the house?" she offered cheerfully. "I think you girls deserve some lunch." The lot of them trailed in a shell-shocked line behind her, casting occasional glances back at the smoking stump as she led the way back to the house.

Rae simply couldn't believe her eyes. She had never seen anything like it before. She had never even imagined it was possible. Even after poring over all her mother's mission files, she had failed to fully grasp a most simple truth.

Her mom was a freaking badass.

She glanced up ahead to where Beth was talking kindly to Molly, trying to coax her out of her daze. "And that's why we didn't bring the car..."

She could almost smell the scorched oak as her mind returned to the kitchen. By this time, Molly and Beth were staring at her with very peculiar looks on their faces.

"Honey, are you alright?" Beth asked with concern.

Molly frowned. "You've been standing there for like, a full minute."

"Yeah, sorry," Rae shook her head quickly and joined them at the table. "So, are we going to find out our actual plan today? Carter said a week, and it's been a week."

Beth rolled up the prints before Rae could get a good look at them. "James is going to tell you all about it after dinner. So for now, I want you to call in the boys, and you kids get yourselves cleaned up. You're all helping me cook tonight. It's a family affair."

"A family affair?" Rae repeated with raised eyebrows. "With...*James*?"

Beth shot her a grin. "Yes, my dear daughter, adults have first names too."

"Oh, I'm well aware of that, *Beth*." Rae rose to the challenge. "Or is that a name that only Devon is allowed to call you? After your secret talk with him that I'm not allowed to know anything about, *because everyone here hates me*?!"

Molly gave her a conspiratorial nudge. "You kind of went off the rails there near the end, but I liked it! Feel the burn!" With that, she skipped up the stairs to claim the first shower.

Rae rolled her eyes, but followed her mother's instructions and headed out to the backyard to call in the boys.

How strange my life has become, she thought to herself as she watched the three of them going through the paces for a moment from the doorway. *It's like I'm in some sort of music video. Like Thriller?!*

And it was true.

There was something about the hearty food and open Scottish air that was taking the already- handsome men to newer, even sexier heights. Maybe it was just the fact that they'd all started wearing less clothing, she mused as she watched them working out. Couldn't really bundle up when going through an obstacle course, could you? Or training with spears and throwing knives? Or just lifting weights in the afternoon sun?

"Enjoying the view?" Devon interrupted her thoughts with a roguish grin.

Rae snapped back at attention only to realize, in utter humiliation, that they were all watching her, giving her the same peculiar look that Molly and Beth had just moments before.

I have got to stop spacing out like this!

"Hey, um, my mom wants you all to get cleaned up and then come downstairs. Apparently, we're all cooking dinner and then Carter is finally going to tell us his secret plan."

"Your mom sent you, huh?" Gabriel teased, coming over and resting his arm on the ledge above her. "Rae, sweetheart, if you want to play, just come right out and ask." He leaned his head down towards hers. "I certainly wouldn't mind going a round or two with you."

He vanished the next moment with a muffled cry, and Rae looked up in shock to see Devon standing where he used to be, holding a blunt club in his hand.

"Oh, I'm sorry, man. I didn't see you there. I was just swinging this bat and then *boom,* right where your head used to be." He tossed it to the ground with a frown. "Bad timing, huh?"

When Gabriel pulled himself to his feet, there was a fire burning in his eyes. "You want to fight, Wardell? I mean—really fight? Be my guest." All trace of a smile was gone as he raised his hands to beckon Devon forward. "I'll bet you don't last two minutes."

The boys took an angry step towards each other, but before they could touch Julian swept in between them, inadvertently pushing both of them away. "Carter's coming," he said innocently.

In a flash, both of them disappeared into the house so fast Rae could have sworn they became invisible.

"Are they *always* like that?" she asked Julian in horror.

He gave her a long-suffering sigh. "Yep."

Her lips twitched into a smile. "Carter's not really coming, is he?"

"Nope."

Cooking actually turned out to be a rather enjoyable affair. Beth and Carter had run in to town to get some wine and cider to go with the meal, so for once all five of them were completely unsupervised and alone.

What could have turned into a disaster, especially based on the behavior Rae had just seen outside, had actually been surprisingly fun.

She supposed it was because, deep down, all of them, even Gabriel, were pretty damn fun people. A constant stream of bloodshed and 'near misses' could only stifle it for so long. They were teenagers, after all. *Teenagers like to goof around.* She thought back to her time early on at Guilder, before people had started trying to kill her and she was expected to save the world. It had been fun. *She* had been fun. All in all, they were some of the best times of her life.

That afternoon had turned out to be more of the same.

"I don't get it," Gabriel had complained, coughing for the millionth time as a thin coat of flour clung to his face. "Rae's a conjurer now, right? Can't she just conjure us some dinner?"

"Oh, but that wouldn't teach us moral fiber," Molly insisted sarcastically, standing atop four thick cooking books just so she could reach the pot to stir.

"And trust me," Julian interjected with a smile, "you don't want to eat anything Rae tried to conjure. It's not exactly one of her strong suits."

Gabriel shot him a grin without seeming to think about it, a grin that escalated to a full-on laugh as Rae popped her head out of the spice cupboard where she'd been searching for cumin.

"Hey, you didn't have any problem with that suit I made you."

Julian shrugged. "Not all conjuring is the same. You're good with stuff. And beer. But no, I wouldn't have eaten the suit."

"It might have been an upgrade from those vanilla cookies," Devon muttered, stabbing a meat thermometer through a leg of turkey.

There was laughter in the kitchen once more.

One by one, some of the barriers that had been keeping them apart slowly broke down. Gabriel, the shameless flirt, the kind who could make you want to tear your hair out, even relaxed. Rae got the feeling that he was a bit of a sweetheart deep down. Very, very deep down.

"Hey, you remember when I told you I wanted to sleep with your girlfriend?" he added to the joking, the laughter still lingering on his face.

"Yeah," Devon said, still laughing.

"That was true."

Devon shot him a stony look, but instead of hitting him with another miniature baseball bat, he just walked calmly forward and reached for the flour to help put it away. Granted, he clapped both sides of the bag, re-exploding it in Gabriel's face first, but it was progress.

But even more than the four of them getting used to Gabriel, Rae had a feeling that the deeper obstacle was Gabriel getting used to them. There was something unexpectedly guarded about him. Something that didn't quite jibe with his otherwise-bright demeanor. More than a lot of openly defensive people she knew, Rae got the feeling that this guy wouldn't let anyone get close. Ever. He might play and tease with the rest of them, but there was something broken there. Deep inside.

It was through that lens that she watched *him*, watch *them* all during dinner. Every time someone cracked a self-deprecating joke, or the table erupted in laughter, his eyes would flash up in surprise for a split second, like he wasn't sure it was real, before he joined in. His mouth opened in actual awe the first time Molly went on one of her famous 'doesn't need to take a breath' speeches about the quality of the sushi place there in town, and when Carter reached over to fondly ruffle Devon's hair after telling a story, Gabriel's eyes locked on every movement like a hawk.

Rae had laughed at the idea before, but it really was a 'family affair.' And although Gabriel was by no means a part of that family yet, he looked like maybe he was getting there. Or at least, maybe he wanted to get there.

But all the laughter and frivolity ended the second Carter joined them at the table after it had been cleared. He unrolled the final map, and without any further pretense started tracing lines with his finger, and emphasizing each stop with a deliberate jab at the paper.

"You'll come in through the tunnels *here*—Rae you'll be invisible. Gabriel—you'll be topside. The guards will lead you down through this corridor *here*, where you'll end up in my office for a formal review. One the review is underway, Rae will sneak up through the ventilation duct, *here*, and make her way into this chamber. That's the place where the piece of the device is kept."

"It's right in there?" Rae repeated tentatively. "In a hidden room behind your office?"

Carter nodded briskly. "From there, it's just a thirty-foot climb through a barred roof to get back to the outside. Actually, it's set up very similarly to your old cell." He shot Rae a faint smile.

"Ha-ha," she answered sarcastically. "Well, that doesn't seem so hard..." She glanced around at her friends, but they seemed as dumbfounded as she was.

Was she missing something here? A room exactly like her cell? The cell that she'd busted out of without so much as breaking a sweat?

"Not so fast, Miss Kerrigan," Carter stopped her. "The room is very much like your old cell, aside from one major difference."

He paused, and she leaned forward anxiously. "And what's that?"

"You won't be able to use any of your tatùs."

Chapter 9

Home sweet home.

Except, for the first time that Rae could remember, it didn't feel like home. Not one little bit.

She trailed invisibly along behind her friends, arms wrapped around Devon's waist as she took care to step only in his footprints. There were too many people with too many powers around here to take any chances. It had been bad enough when Molly accidently shut the door before she'd gotten out of the car like the rest of them. Gabriel had to pretend that he'd left his phone, just to give himself a legitimate reason to open it back up again so she could slip through.

Of course, these kinds of mistakes were to be expected. Rae was hardly infallible. And that brought with it a whole slew of little errors and human faux pas.

On the other hand, these kinds of mistakes could dictate whether she would get caught by Guilder security and spend the rest of her life in prison.

No pressure.

She squeezed Devon's waist and lightly kissed the back of his jacket. He couldn't respond, but she thought she saw the corner of his lip twitch up in a secret, reassuring smile.

That's it, Rae. Breathe. You're just out for a walk with your boyfriend at your old school. No big deal; you've done it a million times.

Of course, on none of those occasions had she been trying to break *in* to the school.

They headed past the main office and took a turn up the bend to get to the Oratory. The secret chambers of the Privy Council were located directly beneath. An unseasonably cold breeze blew Rae's hair in a dark cloud around her and she leaned in closer to Devon with a shiver.

She had indeed made this walk probably a million times. But never before had she fully appreciated the measures of security Guilder employed on behalf of its students. Not only was there the invisible force-field enacted in times of trouble to keep people with tatùs both inside in out, but there were two massive guards posted at the gate; as well as a regular team of at least eight more that kept an eye on the perimeter. Everything inside past a certain level was passcode-protected. Although Rae had joked about it once, there were actual retinal scans and voice-activated doors in the lower levels of the underground chambers. As for the school, not only were there the scores of teenage students, each gifted with super-human potential, training round the clock to hone those skills for the good of the country, but there were the teachers as well. Literal masters of ink.

In short, Guilder was virtually impenetrable. On every level, there were measures in place that would make any sort of incursion nothing short of a suicide mission.

Of course, she had a way around all these measures. A proverbial ace up her sleeve.

Carter.

They'd spent the last three days going over every inch of the grounds and security to an exhaustive degree. She'd stared at the blueprints long enough to make her eyes bleed, and he had instilled in each and every one of them every contingency option known to man.

Yes, there was a plan. And considering how complicated this little endeavor could have been, the plan was surprisingly simple.

While Gabriel was to inconspicuously join the perimeter-protection detail—Julian, Devon, and Molly would walk straight inside of their own volition. Rae would follow along behind, undetected. Once inside, they would willingly surrender themselves to be cross-examined by the President of the Privy Council himself—aka Carter. Thanks to his unique ability to see into the very depths of a person's soul, Carter was the ultimate go-to man for determining the truth of a matter.

Fortunately for Rae, he was also secretly on their side.

No matter what he saw, he would swear to their sincerity, freeing them of all the suspicion they'd naturally garnered since Rae's escape and their subsequent unexplained absence. He would then discreetly trigger the voice-recognition software leading to the chamber, and Rae, once the room was clear, would sneak inside and steal the device.

They could have gone through the main entrance of the Privy Council, but Carter argued it would be too obvious that something was up. Coming this way would make the PC less suspicious, and they needed every little bit of help they could get.

After all this, her only obstacle would be scaling a thirty-foot rock wall to climb through a ceiling crossed by iron bars. Without using any tatùs.

Admittedly, that's where the plan went off the rails a bit.

"See," Carter had said with a wicked smile, "I told you there was a reason I've been having you hang off the rafters for the last seven days. You're going to need those arm muscles if you want to make it out of that chamber without your powers."

Only a sharp kick in the shins from Molly had prevented Rae's cheeky retort.

And now here they were, attempting the impossible. Just a regular Saturday night.

They came to a sudden stop in front of the Oratory, and all five of them took a deep breath. Then Gabriel turned around and stuck his hands in his pockets.

"I'm going to head up for guard patrol," he said with a glance around, hoping to lend as much credence to their story as possible. "But I'm glad the three of you decided to come in.

We're going to need all hands on deck if we want to catch that little traitor."

Rae's eyes narrowed and she could have sworn she saw him wink.

"Anyway, good luck with Carter." He began jogging away up the hill. "I hear he can be a real hard-ass."

Molly watched him go for a minute, before her mouth turned up in disgust. "Yeah, I don't care who hears, I *really* hate that guy."

Devon sighed. "Let's just go in and get this over—"

"Wardell?"

The four of them whirled around in surprise as an enormous man Rae had never seen before came pacing up from around the Oratory. Devon froze for a second, before his face melted into a welcoming smile.

"Hey Brick, I didn't know you were scheduled tonight."

Brick?! Of course his name's Brick.

Rae's eyes widened as they travelled from the tip of the man's muddy work boots to the top of his crew cut. He was even bigger than the bouncer at the bar. Really? The irony of life was sometimes too much. Rae swore if she ever wrote a book about her adventures at Guilder, she'd be using all that irony as foreshadowing.

The man came to a stop in front of them, casually positioning himself between them and the door. "On duty every night until they catch Kerrigan." He squinted ever so slightly as he looked down at them. "And on that note, we haven't seen you three in a while."

Molly shot Devon a quick look, and he cleared his throat quickly. "Yeah, that's uh...why we're here." He pulled himself up to his full height and tried to act as casual as Brick. "We came to submit to voluntary questioning by Carter. I know I speak for all of us when I say I don't want there to be any doubt as to where my loyalties lie."

Brick raised his eyebrows, looking impressed. Apparently, anyone who would willingly allow their boss to know their every thought and secret warranted a good deal of respect.

"Sheesh, man. Well...good for you." The accompanying smile he gave Devon seemed much more relaxed than the first. "I'm serious; it's really good to have you back. When they said *you'd* gone missing, well..." he paused, then jutted up his chin proudly, "I didn't believe any of the rumors. I knew there was no way you'd jump ship. You're more loyal than a dog. Just like me."

The very faintest of shadows flitted across Devon's face, before he cleared it into an easy grin. "Thank, buddy! Well," he sighed dramatically, "we'd better head on inside and get this over and done with."

"Just a minute," Brick put a light but massive hand on Devon's shoulder, bringing him up short. "I hate to do it, but, you know, protocol is protocol. You understand?"

Devon tensed his shoulders, but nodded his head slowly up and down. "Of course. Knock yourself out."

There was a moment's pause where it seemed like nothing was happening, and then Devon's body locked up and Rae finally made the connection as to who Brick really was.

Of course...the human lie-detector.

That was the name he'd earned for himself amongst the guards, but perhaps *lie*-detector was an inaccurate term. It was more like *threat*-detector. She watched in fascination as his ink went into effect. At a glance, it almost looked like Angel's power, but instead of freezing people in place, it was like he slowed them down, like they were moving through thick mud. The time-delay gave him the opportunity he needed for his *real* ink to go into effect: determining whether or not a person presented any sort of danger or threat to the center of his attention. In this case, the Privy Council.

It was an ability that had made him a valuable asset to the Council for many years. Even the stealthiest or most charming suspect couldn't hide the dark motives harbored away in their hearts. Rae could only hope that Devon had enough of a grasp on his bitterness towards the Council for its recent behavior that he didn't send up any red flags.

"Just get on with it," he teased with some difficulty, struggling a bit to speak. "I'm here, alright? Not going anywhere."

Molly and Julian laughed nervously, and even Brick had to smile, before he put his second hand on Devon's other shoulder and moved so they were standing toe to toe.

Then, all they could do was wait.

For a moment, Brick's squinty eyes fogged over, almost like he'd forgotten something and was trying hard to remember what it was.

"What do you say, man?" Devon's grin was fixed on his face. "Do I mean the Privy Council any harm?"

Brick cocked his head and his brows pulled together at the center. This was clearly not the easy read he had been expecting. The longer he took, the more agitated everyone around him became. Julian had actually started to reach for his Taser, when Brick suddenly pulled back, releasing Devon and shaking his head, like he'd come up for air.

"Sorry about that, man, it's just..." He shook his head some more, trying to clear it. "You've got a real mess of feelings going on in there."

Devon straightened his jacket briskly and avoided eye contact. "Well, Kerrigan was one of my oldest friends and we did go through a lot together. It's hard to believe she had her father's intentions at heart. Hey, you think you know a person, but you really don't. I certainly don't mean the Council any harm."

"No," Brick agreed seriously, "no, you don't. Well, good luck, you guys. I'll radio in to let them know you're coming."

"Thanks." Devon clapped Brick quickly on the shoulder as the four of them made their way inside. Molly and Julian avoided touching him altogether.

Once they were inside the Oratory itself, the level of 'creepy surreal' soared to whole new heights. As Rae looked around the familiar carved walls, there was a strange, almost guilty tightening in her chest. She had basically grown up in here. In all the ways that mattered. *Coming of age.* And now here she was, breaking in like some sort of criminal.

It's not your fault, she reminded herself as they walked noiselessly to the hidden doors set into the far wall. *Everything you've ever done has been to protect them. It's they who turned their backs on you.*

For whatever reason, that didn't make the feeling go away. In fact, it only made it worse.

They slipped through the first of the doors without a problem and were headed down the main underground hall, when Devon suddenly stopped short. His eyes flicked toward the stone wall, and a hint of a smile pulled up the corner of his lips.

"Jesse," he said, with a curt nod of his head.

Rae stared at the stones in bewilderment, and then stifled an actual shriek of surprise as the slender body of a young man pulled away from the rocks.

"How did you know it was me?" he asked with a grin. Before their very eyes, his coloration took on that of a normal college kid, the expert camouflage of the wall melting away.

Devon grinned back and clapped him good-naturedly on the back. "Your breathing. Rocks don't breathe."

The boy named Jesse shook his head, looking slightly frustrated. "Yeah, I haven't been able to work that part out yet."

"You will," Devon said encouragingly. He stepped back to allow Jesse and Julian to shake hands. "Just give it time."

The kid grinned again. "Too bad your old partner's not around to help me. I heard it only takes her a minute to master someone's ink and then..." His voice trailed off as Devon's face tightened and turned away. "Hey, man, I'm sorry. I still can't believe she got arrested. That sucks."

Still invisible to the rest of the world, Rae smirked with satisfaction. At least *someone* who worked here thought so. And damn if she didn't want to reach out and touch Jessie to mimic his tatù. Now wasn't the time, but maybe one day...

"Uh...thanks," Devon said quickly. "Hey listen, we've got to run. Is Carter in his office?"

For the first time, Jesse looked a bit nervous. "Yeah, with about half the rest of the Council. Brick radioed that you were coming in, and everyone raced down to watch your little interrogation."

"That's just...perfect," Julian muttered darkly, staring down the dimly-lit hall.

Jesse's eyes flicked down the hall as well before he took a few steps back, melting into a colorful painting of Henry VIII mounted on the wall. "Good luck. You might need it."

"Thanks," Devon murmured, leading them forward once more.

The closer they got to the office, the harder Rae's heart began pounding in her chest.

What the hell had they been thinking?! Sneaking in to the Privy Council?! They'd been stopped twice already, and they hadn't even made it to Carter yet. Who knew how many more super-human guards were waiting just around the next corner? What if someone had the power to see people who were invisible? Both Devon and Carter had assured her that wasn't the case, but what if she just bumped into someone? With half the Council gathered in Carter's small office, it wasn't exactly unlikely...

And if she did? Well, it would be back to the holding cell and then off to start her new life in prison the very next morning.

Almost as if sensing her fright, Devon slipped his hands casually into his jacket pockets, giving her fingers a gentle squeeze as he did. She pulled in a silent breath and tried to slow down her racing pulse.

Devon would never let that happen. He'll never let me go back to jail. Hell, I'd never let me go back to jail. We'll just stick to the plan, and everything will be fine.

But all those good feelings went right out the window when Julian opened the door to Carter's office.

It wasn't half the Council waiting on the other side. It was the whole bloody thing.

The four friends froze in place as the eyes of forty or so stern-looking men latched onto them with terrifying attention. Molly's already-pale face turned even whiter, and Julian reached down to silently take her hand. Still hiding behind Devon, Rae had stopped breathing.

Carter sat at the center of it all, and it was on him that Rae focused all her energy. Carter was on their side. Carter would see them through this. He had to.

"I'm sorry, sir," Devon's voice sounded as small as Rae had ever heard it. "We didn't mean to interrupt—"

Carter held up a hand to silence him, the hard lines on his face making him look especially grim. "Not at all, Mr. Wardell. Actually, the Council has gathered here today for you three. To hear what you and your two friends have to say."

Mr. Wardell. Just a few days before, Carter and Devon had been sharing a secret bottle of scotch, telling war stories in front of a bonfire in Scotland. Now it was *Mr. Wardell.*

Rae jumped with the rest of them as the door behind them suddenly slammed shut and locked.

Devon tried to keep his composure, nodding quickly and pulling himself together. "Alright, well, that's why we're here."

"And why is that, exactly?" a ferocious-looking man demanded from a few chairs away. He had a tuft of white hair clinging to the top of his head, and beady black eyes that seemed to have no color around them whatsoever. "Perhaps to explain where the three of you have been these last few days? Or perhaps to explain your previous absence for the entire month after Guilder's graduation?"

His harsh words echoed in the little room and Devon pulled in a quick breath.

No...this was not going to be as easy as they thought. Not that they had even thought it would be.

"My friends and I took a leave of absence after graduation. It was fully sanctioned by the Council, and Carter was fully aware that we were going. I regret that I didn't tell you where exactly we went." His voice sharpened slightly. "As we weren't on active assignment, I didn't realize it was in the Council's purview to track our every movement."

A low murmur hissed through the room, and sitting behind his desk, Carter shook his head a fraction of an inch. This was not the man to be messing with. Devon needed to pull back.

The man in question, however, seemed to literally rise to the occasion. His withered old body looked to almost re-inflate as he half-rose from his chair and pointed a gnarled finger at Devon's chest. "You, young man, are a multi-million dollar, malfunctioning asset. Nothing more. From the minute you graduated and signed your employment contract, you became the Council's living, breathing property. Everything you do is within our purview. Everywhere you go, everything you think. You are no longer your own person. You belong to something greater." His voice fell to a dangerous whisper, "Do you understand?"

An icy chill ran down Rae's back and she realized she was trembling where she stood. Carter was right: Cromfield had been working to undermine the Council since before anyone in this room was even born. And, upon hearing those words, it seemed he was well on his way.

Property of the Council?! A malfunctioning asset?!

He was making it sound like some kind of cult! Like they'd signed their entire lives away!

She could feel Devon stiffen in front of her. In a way, she was almost glad she couldn't see his face. She couldn't imagine what it must look like right now.

There was a brief pause, and then he inclined his head, lowering his voice to a more respectful tone. "Yes, sir."

"I couldn't hear you, *boy*!"

He lifted his chin and Rae could practically see the fire burning in his eyes. "Yes. Sir."

The man lowered himself back down to his chair. "Good. Now, where have the three of you been since Miss Kerrigan's convenient escape from the detention center?"

Convenient escape? Rae's eyes flicked nervously to her three friends, each one standing stiff as a board in front of her. Maybe this wasn't the greatest idea after all. This man was out for blood.

"We were in Liverpool, sir," Julian answered in a soft voice, "where I grew up."

The lethal-looking man turned his snake-eyes to Julian. "Liverpool..." He rifled through some papers, presumably, Julian's file. "You spent time in foster care there, correct?"

Rae's mouth dropped open in shock, and Molly shot Julian a look of total bewilderment.

He'd never really talked about his family, his life at home. But Rae had never for a moment assumed that was because he had problems!

"Yes, sir," he answered in that same obedient tone. "I was thirteen when then-President Axe came to collect me. My father had gone missing while working for the Privy Council, and my mother couldn't manage. I spent some time in foster care. When my MIA father returned, President Axe came and took me to Guilder."

He had done well to mention Carter's predecessor—Rae could tell. She wanted to ask him a million questions but there was a reason he hadn't mentioned his childhood and it wasn't her place to ask unless he wanted to tell. There was another general murmur throughout the room, but this time it was a far lighter tone. The man had been liked, and this boy was apparently part of his collection.

Even old snake-eyes had to agree. "President Axe was a good man, God rest him."

Julian kept his eyes on the floor. "Yes, sir. He was."

"And the three of you, all three of you were in Liverpool after Miss Kerrigan's escape?"

"We wanted to get a little distance," Molly piped up, looking terrified to be speaking for the first time. "Rae is...well, *was* my best friend. She was close to all of us. We needed to get a little space. We'd hoped that by the time we came back she would have been found already and brought back."

Even though she knew the words were fake, Rae couldn't help but feel stung. Molly had said them so convincingly, talking about her in the past tense as though she was already gone. It was nothing compared to what she felt when Devon spoke next.

"And you, Mr. Wardell?" The man turned back to him. "You have no further loyalties to Miss Kerrigan?"

Rae expected Devon to sigh. For him to hang his head, maybe wring his hands; somehow act like it was a difficult question for him. What she didn't expect him to do was smile.

"You just said it yourself, sir. She's a *Kerrigan*."

It felt like a knife had been plunged straight into Rae's heart. Her whole body seemed to lock down, and she took a silent step back.

"I'd hoped she might turn out to be different from her father," he continued, speaking in that same quiet monotone that was breaking Rae's heart. "When I was assigned to be her mentor at Guilder, I thought she showed some promise. That she believed in our way of thinking, like her mother. But she turned out to be exactly the same as what we had been told about her father."

Two invisible tears snuck down Rae's face and she was quick to catch them before they hit the floor. *He's lying,* she told herself. *You know he's lying, so get it together.*

However, there was something horrible about seeing him standing there, calmly tearing her entire life apart. It chilled her to the bone. *Like he expected her to turn into her father.* It hurt something fierce. She took another step away from him. Maybe her father had been brainwashed by Cromfield. Maybe he wasn't really bad, but the Privy Council had assumed he wasn't worth saving and, in fact, led him in the direction of her downfall. She glared at each member in the room, her eyes resting lastly on Carter. He was in love with her mother. Maybe he too had pushed Simon away with the hope of having a future with Beth. The thought shocked her. She forced herself to focus on what Devon was saying, not on what- ifs and could-have-beens.

Devon hung his head and sighed, "I admit I was still disappointed. It's one of the reasons I went with Julian and Molly when they suggested we get out of town for a while to clear our heads." Then his voice grew stronger and he looked the scary old man right in the eyes. "But my loyalty is, and has always been, to the Council. I wouldn't risk that for Miss Kerrigan. I wouldn't risk it for anything in the world."

The man sat back in his chair, looking satisfied, and made a subtle gesture to Carter. With a slight nod, Carter got to his feet and motioned the three of them forward. "As much as we appreciate your words, there is nothing like the truth." He held his hands out and beckoned them. "It's time to prove it."

As Molly, Julian, and Devon made their way slowly across the room, Rae slipped around to the back, hugging her way around the wall until she was directly behind Carter's desk. Once she was there, she pulled in a deep breath and wiped her teary eyes.

He didn't mean it. None of them did. They'd just done it so convincingly. It's time to pull it all together, Rae. We're here for a reason. I'm the next one up at bat.

The entrance to the chamber was supposedly in the hearth behind his chair. And as much as she didn't want to be anywhere near her friends as they went through this next part, she had to be close enough to open the door in the brief window where the lock would be deactivated.

She watched as, one by one, her friends stepped forward and took Carter's hand. It was impossible to tell what was going on behind their faces, or if Carter was even using his tatù at all. At first, Rae suspected he wasn't, because Molly had a slightly over-theatrical reaction; squinting her eyes shut with a look of concentration that was most unlike her. Things were different with Julian. There was a hesitation in the way he presented his hand to Carter, followed by a knowing gleam in Carter's eye as he probed deep into the boy's thoughts.

Well, that's one way to find out about Angel. Carter did say they'd discuss it later...

Finally, there was just Devon left. He stepped forward slowly, and Rae realized that she was holding her breath. The last time Carter had used his ability on Devon, it had been the day that he professed his undying love. Just moments before, Carter had admitted that he'd been using his ink to spy on Devon and Rae's progressing relationship. It had been such an explosive confrontation; the two men had almost come to blows. But instead, Devon had merely held out his arm and asked Carter to tell him if what he felt, in all its purity, could possibly be wrong.

It was the first time Rae had ever seen Carter cry.

Devon held his arm out again, this time with a little knowing smile dancing deep behind his eyes. Carter touched his skin and both of them bowed their heads for the briefest of moments. Free from the sight of the hushed crowd, Rae stuck her hands on her hips and rolled her eyes, staring between them with a sarcastic little smile.

Carter wasn't doing a damn thing. Devon had forbidden it after that day at Heath Hall.

After a minute, Carter gave Devon's wrist a little squeeze and both men lifted their heads.

"Let the record reflect that I, James Carter, have knowingly and thoroughly—"

There was an almost-inaudible click behind her as the lock to the chamber temporarily de-activated at the sound of Carter's name. Moving as quietly as she could, Rae pried the little door open using nothing but her fingernails, hoping it would be enough to keep it from locking shut.

"—investigated the minds of all the accused. They are indeed," he paused for effect, "free and clear of all suspicion. They are all now, and have been always, loyal to the Council."

There was a much louder reaction through the crowd at the news. Some people smiled with open applause. Others looked strangely disappointed. Snake-eyes just stared unblinkingly forward.

"As such, I believe it's time we put them back to work." Carter gave Devon a stern, yet teasing, smile. "I believe your 'leave of absence' has been long enough."

Devon ginned back, following along behind Carter as he led the crowd slowly from the room. The rest of the men stood and followed suit, several of them patting Molly and Julian on the back as they filed out into the hall. Eventually, there was only old snake-eyes left.

He hadn't moved from his chair since Carter had pronounced their innocence. In fact, he hadn't stopped staring at the wall directly behind Carter's chair. The exact same spot where Rae was currently standing, not daring to breathe, with her fingernails still wedged in the door.

What looked to be the ghost of a smile lifted the corners of his ancient lips, and for a moment the noise from the hall seemed to dim, leaving the office a deathly quiet.

I'm caught. I'm so dead. He's going to scream that I'm here. All my friends are going to be put in jail. Carter in the cell beside us. What the—

Then Carter looked back inside and called, "Victor, are you coming?"

In one brisk motion, the man pushed to his feet, placing his bowler hat firmly back on his head and heading outside with the rest of them. The door shut firmly behind him, and for what felt like the first time in hours, Rae took a deep breath.

Damn it!!

Finally! She thought she was going to stroke out from the stress of it all.

Now for the hard part...

She turned again to the hidden door, and moving as quietly as she could, she slowly pulled it back to reveal a small stone cavern on the other side. It was dark, save for the pale glow of moonlight shining down from above, with a tiny stone column rising up from the center.

Sitting upon the column, shining faintly in the silver glow, was the missing piece.

Rae sucked in another quick breath and prepared herself for what was going to be a grueling climb. She'd come to rely upon her powers so much that being in this 'dead zone,' she literally had no idea what to expect. Would she even be able to pull herself out of there to where Gabriel was waiting for her at the top?

You have to. Everything depends on it.

With a silent prayer for strength, she took a deep breath and steeled her nerves. She took a step into the cold, small room, and gazed up through the bars at the full moon.

She was still marveling at how ironically peaceful it was when an alarm began screaming, the frequency high-pitched and near her ear.

Chapter 10

NO, NO, NO! PLEASE NO! NOT NOW!

There was a distant crash and a series of shouts, but by the time Rae could turn around to look, the stone door to the chamber had already locked shut.

"Devon?!" she screamed, pounding on the wall. "Molly?! Jules?!"

The alarm didn't have to do with her in the room. It had to do with those outside the office. Her friends.

Strangely enough, when the second the door was closed she could no longer hear anything of the commotion she knew was happening on the other side. What the hell had just happened? Had they subdued all her friends so quickly?!

She pressed her ear to the door in panic, but it was then that she realized.

This was thick stone. Of course she couldn't hear through it.

And she didn't have her powers anymore.

"Well, that's just *perfect*!" she screamed out, giving the stone another useless punch.

Of all the moments to get locked in a tatù-proof room. It had to be precisely when her three best friends in the whole world just got outed as traitors in front of the entire Privy Council!

Despite all their contingency training, none of them had ever prepared for this. To be frank, the risk in this plan had been Rae's alone. No matter whether or not she was successful, the others would always have been able to walk out the door scot-free. But this...?!

Where had that alarm come from anyway?! Carter had laid out every inch of the compound and this was in his own damn office! What?! He'd forgotten he placed a trip-wire behind the door?!

A loud noise from behind her made her whirl around again, only to see that the column supporting the missing piece was sinking slowly back into the earth.

"What is this?! Indiana Jones?!" she shrieked, darting forward to get it.

She was able to snatch it up just before it disappeared entirely, and stood there in a breathless panic, clutching it to her chest as she stared up at the sky.

What the hell was she supposed to do now?! How the hell was she supposed to just walk away from here, knowing that there was a three-on-forty fight going on right outside the chamber?!

First thing's first, Rae. Get the hell out of this hole so you can use your powers!

After securing the device inside a leather strap wound tightly across her chest, she darted to the wall and grabbed onto the first jagged edge she could find.

It was *nothing* like doing it with powers. Her body ached and strained in protest, and by the time she was only a few feet up, her arms were shaking like branches in the wind.

"Hang for hours from the rafters, he said."

One hand in front of the other, higher and higher.

"It'll make you so much stronger, he said." She was sweating now, little trickles pouring through her long hair as she spoke through clenched teeth.

"And don't worry, it's not like there's a *freaking trip-wire*!"

Her hand slipped and she swung out into the open air with a shriek.

"Rae?!"

She squinted up in alarm as her fingers struggled to find a new grip. "Gabriel? Is that you?!" She could have hugged him with relief if he'd been within arm's reach.

Even silhouetted through the bars, she saw his face break into a wide grin. "We have got to stop meeting like this."

"Would you shut up for once?!" she demanded, inching her way ever higher. "Did you not hear the freaking alarm go off? The others were still down there! We've got to go back—"

"The others are going to be fine," he said calmly, abruptly shifting tone as he registered her blind panic. He knelt down and laced his fingers through the bars. "I may not like your terrible boyfriend, but I have to admit when it comes to this stuff, even I have to respect him. Devon wouldn't have gone in there unprepared. They're going to be fine."

Rae shook her head, her eyes swimming with tears as she struggled to hold on. "But the entire Council was there, Gabriel! How can they fight their way out of—"

"They're going to be fine," he repeated firmly. "Trust me. What we need to do right now is worry about you. Watch your left foot. That ledge is crumbling."

She glanced down in fright to see that he was right. With a strained gasp, she yanked herself up to a higher perch and then paused to take a rest. She was about halfway up now, but her body was rigid with fright and stress and the physical shock of not having her powers. It felt like all of her muscles had completely atrophied, leaving her weak and alone. Without bothering to feel embarrassed, she leaned her forehead into the rocks, panting and crying, unable to think until she knew what was happening on the other side of that wall.

"Gabriel..." she whispered. "I can't lose them. They're my family."

For a moment, his face froze. Then it tightened in determination and he re-doubled his efforts. "And we can't lose you. I mean—*they* can't lose you. Listen to me... Rae!"

He waited until she forced herself to look up at his face. It was gleaming silver in the moonlight, his beautiful green eyes boring into hers with every word he said, "We are going to make it through this. I promise you that." He paused again and measured her expression. "Do you believe me?"

Somehow, as she stared up into his eyes, Rae found that she did. She may not particularly like Gabriel sometimes but, for whatever reason, she trusted him. Trusted *in* him. He would keep his promise. She had no doubts about that. And he would protect her.

After what seemed like a long time, she finally jerked her head up and down. "Yes. I believe you."

He flashed the faintest of smiles before growing serious again. "Good. Now, the first thing we have to do is get you up out of that hole. How are your arms holding up?"

"Not—not good." They were shaking uncontrollably. "Gabriel, I can't hold on much longer."

"Then it's a good thing you're already over halfway there." There was a note of sternness and authority in his voice. "You're stronger than you think." She realized with a start that it was the same kind of voice Devon had used when he was first training her back at Guilder. "Now stop feeling sorry for yourself, Kerrigan, and let's go. There's a crevice about a foot above your right hand, try to reach it."

And so it was. He guided her up, foot by foot, inch by inch. It was excruciating work, but eventually she made it to the top.

Once she was there, she was able to see his face better in the light. Up close, he was sweating just as much as she was, secretly petrified the whole time that she would fall.

"Hey," she gestured to the iron bars with a grin, "get me out of here—okay?" She could feel her tatù itching to come back to full power.

He laughed. "I'm on it."

Without another word, one hand waved carelessly over the bars as the other reached down for her. Except...nothing happened. With a frown, he ignored her for a second and lifted his other hand, running both of them slowly over the bars as Rae clung to the rock directly beneath.

"Why isn't anything happening?" she gasped, panting with the growing strain.

For the first time all night, his face went shock-white. "I don't know. This has never happened to me before." Then it clicked "Except..."

"Except what?" she demanded, struggling to readjust her grip.

"Rae...the bars are part of the chamber. No tatùs in the chamber."

All the air rushed out of her chest in one big *whoosh*.

"So that's it?" Her voice rose in panic. "I'm stuck in here—"

"No," his brow furrowed in concentration as he leaned his entire body into the iron, closing his eyes in concentration. Eventually, a few of them began to shimmer and seemed to shrink just marginally in size. He pulled back, panting. "The bottom half of each bar is in the chamber—power-proof. But the top half is in the open air. If I can just weaken them enough, maybe I can kick my way through."

Rae's fingers slipped again on the slick rock and she gasped as she steadied herself. "Well, please do it in the next ten seconds, because there's no way I can hang on."

"Cool. No pressure."

But behind the joke, he looked sincerely nervous. He kept glancing between her trembling fingers and the wavering bars. Before long, his own hands started shaking from the strain of pushing his ink so far. But no matter how fast he worked, no matter how much he tried, it quickly became clear to both people that there was no way Rae was getting out of this hole in time.

"Gabriel," she said softly.

He ignored her, running his hands again and again over the slowly shrinking bars.

"Gabriel," she tried again, "take the piece."

His eyes darted down to her in shock. "What? Rae, I am NOT giving up on you!"

"And I'm not asking you to. But in case this doesn't work, we need to at least get the piece out of here before Cromfield can come and steal it. Otherwise, all of this was for nothing."

His face tightened in indecision, but she was sure.

"Take it," she said again, stronger this time. "It's on the strap."

It was a testament to the graveness of the situation that Gabriel didn't make a single joke as he reached down through the bars and gently took the device from her chest. His fingers brushed against her bare skin, trying to pull it free whilst not groping her, until eventually, it came loose.

He held it up for just a split second—his eyes flicking between it and Rae's face—before he slipped it quickly into his pocket.

Rae didn't know exactly why, maybe it was because there was a chance she was about to fall and break her neck, maybe it was because Gabriel might be the last person she saw before she spent the rest of her life in prison, but she felt like there was something she needed to say. "Gabriel—"

"So," a familiar voice interrupted, "I leave you alone for five minutes, and you're already trying to cop a feel?"

"Devon!" Rae's heart just about exploded in happiness. "How on earth did you get up here?! I thought for sure you guys were—"

"I brought along a couple contingencies of my own in case things didn't go our way." He grinned breathlessly as he knelt beside Gabriel in the grass. "Aerosol fluothane. They're going to be out for another two minutes. I'm afraid I had to get Carter too, but..." His voice trailed off as he registered their predicament for the first time. "Why are these bars still here?" he asked Gabriel accusingly.

Gabriel gritted his teeth as he continued running his hands over the melting metal. "It's the chamber; it's effecting my power too—"

"RAE!"

Devon shouted into the night as her fingers slipped silently off the ledge.

He dropped down onto his chest and caught her in the nick of time. They watched together as both of her shoes fell off, dropping noiselessly before clattering against the hard ground. "Gabriel—hurry the hell up!" he commanded, before his voice instantly softened to honeyed tones. "Rae, sweetheart, you have to hang on, okay? Can you do that for me? You just need to—"

His voice cut off in a sharp cry and he buried his face in his arm to silence it.

"Devon?!" she shrieked in fright, dangling thirty feet in the air. "What's happened?"

A few drops of blood dripped down onto her face, and Rae immediately understood the problem.

Devon's powers didn't work down here either, and she was holding onto his mangled, recently dislocated arm.

Her mind raced as their fingers struggled to keep hold. "Where's Julian?"

Devon gritted his teeth, trying to keep the pain off his face so as not to worry her. "He's getting the car with Molly. We thought you'd be there already. I... I... I only came here to see what was taking so long."

She slipped an inch down and they both yelled at the same time, "GABRIEL!"

"I'm trying!" he shouted back, putting every ounce of strength he had into his tatù. "Just give me another minute and I'll do it."

Another bloody minute...?

Rae looked up at Devon and her eyes filled with tears. Would he make it that long? Would she? Would the entire Privy Council come to and then find them here like this?

"I can't believe this is happening," she murmured, barely hanging on. "Can this year turn into any more of a nightmare? Damn it!"

"Hey, honey, it's—" both Devon and Gabriel started at the same time.

Devon shot Gabriel a dark, silencing look before he continued speaking alone. "We're going to be fine, okay? I promise. We're going to make it through this, and we're going to go back to the house in Scotland, and we're going to have a ton of sex *really loud* so that this idiot has to hear it..."

Even Gabriel had to smile at the audacity of that one, and Rae giggled weakly.

"...and everything is going to be fine," Devon finished through gritted teeth. "I promised you once that I was going to give you the life you always wanted. I intend to keep that promise. You just need to hold on for me, okay?"

Her hands trembled uncontrollably, but she nodded. "Okay."

In the distance, Rae thought she heard a series of muffled voices coming closer. Devon, who could hear them just fine with his ink, paled a little before turning to Gabriel. "Seriously, man, how much longer?"

Gabriel was just as pale, giving it everything he had. "A few... more... seconds..."

There was a muffled crack; a crack that Rae was horrified to realize had come from Devon's arm, and she slipped another few inches down his wrist. "Devon?!"

"It's okay," he winced, eyes closed. His fingers jerked and trembled, but they tightened painfully around her arm. "It's—" He sucked in a quick gasp and another spatter of blood fell to the floor. "*Shit*—Gabriel, hurry!"

"Come on, baby! Please don't let go," Rae whimpered, willing herself not to look down at the thirty-foot drop beneath her.

"There! It's done!" Gabriel vanished the rest of the bars in triumph.

At that moment, several things happened at once.

Rae's hand slipped out of Devon's at the precise moment his slipped out of hers. In what felt like slow motion, she began to fall—a silent scream coming to her lips as her hair streamed up around her. In that same moment, Gabriel shoved Devon out of the way, and reached into the cavern himself. He caught her by the tips of her fingers and held on for all his worth.

"Damn you, Kerrigan!" he panted, tightening his grip. "I've got you!"

Without a shattered arm to contend with, Gabriel was able to pull her out of the hole in a matter of seconds. Rae's tatù clicked instantly back to life. It turned out to be not a moment too soon. The second they were all top-side, they saw several dark shapes rushing towards them in the distance.

"Come on!" Gabriel yelled, pushing the others forward. "We've got to go!"

Nobody needed to be told twice.

Without looking back, the three of them tore over the lawn. They passed several scattered guards along the way, curtesy of Julian and Molly. By the time they reached the gate, Julian's Jaguar was already revving and ready to go.

They leapt inside, all three in the back.

Rae grabbed Devon's good hand and screamed, "DRIVE!" at the same time Gabriel yelled it and grabbed her other hand.

The car tore off into the night.

Chapter 11

"We're fugitives...we're fugitives..." Molly whimpered for the millionth time, wringing her little hands as she stared out the window. She'd been looping since they left Guilder, unable to stop.

"Are you sure you don't need to go to a hospital?" Rae asked Devon in a low voice, helping him carefully out of his shirt to see the damage beneath.

"Remember what I told you about getting blood on my upholstery..." Julian warned from the driver's seat. Rae shot him a death look and he amended, "...it couldn't matter less."

"...fugitives..."

"I don't need to go to the hospital—and we can't, anyway," Devon winced as he glanced down at the torn skin and bruised muscle. "I just popped it back out of place, that's all. Julian can fix it in a minute when he pulls over."

Gabriel leaned hesitantly forward. "I could fix it right now."

Devon's eyes locked on his. "No."

"Dev," Rae murmured, "this is no time to be proud." She looked at her hand. "Where is all this blood coming from? That's not from a dislocated shoulder."

"I re-opened a few stitches, that's all. Stop worrying, please. I'm fine, I promise."

"Hey, uh, not to interject, but...does anyone want to tell me where I'm going?" Julian called from the front seat.

"We're a little busy back here, Jules," Rae shot back.

"Take your time. I'll just keep lapping the city..."

"...freakin' *fugitives*..."

"Dude, just let me fix it," Gabriel said again.

"Not a chance."

"Why not?" Rae asked sharply.

"One, because he doesn't have a medical degree."

She threw up her hands. "Julian doesn't have a medical degree."

"Yeah, but I watched it three times on YouTube," he called from the front.

Devon nodded seriously. "And I trust that."

Rae rolled her eyes. "And two?"

"Two..." Devon looked Gabriel up and down. "Because he would like it too much."

Gabriel glanced down with a chuckle. "Can't argue with that."

"Enough!" Rae blew back her hair in exasperation. "Gabriel—fix it. Now."

With a victorious smirk, Gabriel leaned across Rae and anchored his hands on Devon's chest and shoulder. Then, with surprisingly merciful efficiency and precision, he snapped it back into place. Devon cried out in pain, before falling back in his seat, cradling it tenderly in his other arm.

"You're right," Gabriel grinned, leaning back in his own seat, "I liked that way too much."

"Heaven help us..." Rae moaned, burying her face in her hands.

Julian piped up again, "Yeah, uh, not to keep harping on it, but we've crossed the bridge like five times now and I'm running out of gas. Do we have any sort of destination in mind?"

"Just pick a place and park," Devon groaned, leaning his head against the window.

"Hey, do you think you could conjure us up some coffee?" Gabriel asked suddenly.

"...legit, on the run, fugitives..."

"*Okay, that's it!*" Rae yelled. "*Julian, stop the car!*"

Five heads lurched to a stop as they swung suddenly up against the curb.

"Thank..." Rae started to say. Then her voice trailed off as she realized where they were.

"What the hell are we doing here?" Devon asked in alarm, staring up at the swanky London penthouse. "Get us out of here, Jules!"

"Nice place," Gabriel commented appreciatively. He turned to Rae with a wink. "Yours?"

Rae glanced up and down the street in fright. "Seriously, Julian! *Anywhere* but here!"

But Julian merely shook his head and got out of the car. The others scrambled after him in dismay, all in various states of worry and panic.

"Jules, have you lost your freaking—"

"They won't come here," he said simply. "They think it's too obvious and that we wouldn't dare. In no possible future do they come here."

In a sign of the utmost respect of his skills, no one said another word about it.

Instead, Molly looked longingly up at her once-and-future home, before turning to Rae with a teary sigh. "...Rae?"

"Yeah, Molls?"

Molly's lip quivered as she finally said the words for the last time.

"We're all on the Council's hit list now. All of us. Fugitives."

Standing in the middle of the darkened London street that night, the five of them finally paused their perpetual forward motion and shared a most peculiar look.

Then Rae turned to her little friend and clapped her gently on the shoulder.

"Welcome to the club. We'll get matching strait jackets."

"Well, I love what you've done with the place." Gabriel laughed as he looked around at the bare walls and stacked boxes.

"Yeah, well," Rae helped lower Devon down into a chair, "I've been a little busy trying to thwart a psychopath and then break out of jail."

He clucked his tongue and shook his head. "A good housekeeper knows there are no excuses for shabby work."

"What are you? Martha Stewart?"

"That reference doesn't work here, America."

She rolled her eyes and turned back to Devon. "Come on, sweetie. Let's get you into the shower. Molls, do we have hot water in this place yet? Uh...where's the bathroom again?"

Molly lifted her hand to point, but Devon cut her off.

"Not before we talk about what the hell happened back there." He was pale from the loss of blood, but determined to see it through. "Since when was there a trip-wire alarm set behind Carter's desk? He never said a *word* about that."

"He couldn't have known," Julian said, taking a seat behind him. "When the thing went off, he was as surprised as the rest of us were. In fact, he actually knocked out Carlton and Blanchard from behind so you could set off the gas."

Gabriel remained quiet—looking at them with troubled eyes.

"So where does that leave us?" Rae asked in frustration. "Someone else put it there without Carter's knowledge? Meaning someone inside the Privy Council suspects *Carter* now? It doesn't make any sense."

A loud throat cleared from the corner, and they turned to look at Molly.

"Let me be the first to say, *I no longer care.*" She sighed in exhaustion. "So something else went tragically wrong. Honestly, at this point, did anyone expect anything different? The bars wouldn't move, Devon broke his arm again, Julian got caught in a trance and fell into a fountain—"

"Wait...what?" Devon asked curiously, turning to look at his blushing friend.

"The *point* is, instead of clearing our names, we're freaking fugitives! So I'm not dealing with it—I'm not going to try to puzzle it out. I'm done." Molly's bright eyes flashed as she stared at them. "We're not going to get any answers until we can talk to Carter, and we're not going to be able to do that any time soon. So in the meantime, I'm going to forget about the Privy Council, and try to enjoy what will probably be the only night I ever get to have in my own freaking apartment!"

In a blur of auburn hair, she hopped back down and held out her hand in front of Rae.

"Vodka," she demanded, with no further explanation.

Rae very calmly conjured a glass for Molly, and they all watched as she stomped across the tiled floor and slammed the door to her bedroom.

Her words and the frustration behind left a profound effect on the room, and no one spoke for a long time afterwards. It was several minutes before Gabriel finally glanced at Julian.

"You fell in a fountain?"

Julian flushed, and gestured to his dripping clothes. "This whole time, none of you guys wondered why I was wet?"

Gabriel and Rae stifled a smile while Devon gave him a painful shrug. "You didn't wonder why I was covered in blood," he countered.

Julian conceded with a yawn. "Honestly, you're usually like that now. I think maybe your dad was right; ever since you started hanging out with this one," he gave Rae a nod, "you're always all messed up from something or another."

"Thanks, Jules," Rae said scathingly, but he shot her a grin and she had to smile.

Gabriel watched the entire exchange with a rather strange expression on his face. His eyes flicked from Molly's closed door, to Julian and Rae's lighthearted teasing, to Devon slowly bleeding onto the new couch.

"You guys have really been through a lot together, haven't you?" he asked softly.

Rae turned to him in surprise, but the other two boys seemed too fatigued to notice his sudden change in tone.

"It's something you get used to," Julian said distractedly, wringing his sleeve onto the floor.

Devon flinched as he flexed out his arm. "It's not like we really had a choice. Cromfield's insane—he's a murderous freaking psychopath." His eyes leveled on Rae. "And he happens to be after the one thing that matters most to me in the whole world."

"He means *me*," Julian whispered loudly.

But Devon had locked eyes suddenly with Gabriel, staring at him like he'd just noticed he was sitting there for the first time. "And on that note..."

He stood up so suddenly that Rae jumped up as well. Gabriel took a step instinctively backwards—probably afraid he was about to get hit. But Devon didn't hit him. Instead, he crossed the room and did the last thing that anyone present would have ever expected.

Devon gave Gabriel a hug.

Gabriel froze dead still, staring at Rae over Devon's shoulder with wide eyes.

"*What the hell is happening right now?*" he muttered. He glanced at Devon nervously, "You don't...like...have a knife on you or something, right?"

Devon chuckled, but when he pulled away he couldn't have looked more sincere. "I wanted to thank you. Back in the cavern when...when you caught her." His eyes travelled over to Rae, and an automatic smile warmed his face. A smile that still lingered when he turned back to Gabriel. "She's my whole..." He shook his head. "Anyway—thank you. I mean it."

Gabriel shifted a bit uncomfortably, like he had never been on the receiving end of a hug before. "I think you lost a bit too much blood, my friend," he joked, trying to shift the attention.

Devon grinned and clapped him on the shoulder. "I'm serious, man. You'll get no more complaints from me. And if there's ever anything I can do for you, please don't hesitate to—"

"You could let me sleep with your girlfriend..."

Devon's smile faltered a moment as Rae covered her face. His hands clenched into momentary fists before he smoothed them out and said, "Look, I'm really trying here—"

"I know, I know," Gabriel cut him off with a genuine smile of his own. Rae suspected that Devon's little speech touched him more than he let on. "I'm just messing with you. And it's cool, about before. Anything I can do to help."

Without thinking about it, he clapped Devon cheerfully in return...on his torn shoulder.

"*Son of a—*"

It was a testament to how physically, mentally, and emotionally exhausting the day had been that they were able to get even a wink of sleep that night.

Of course, the last hours of the evening hadn't exactly helped. Julian had downed half a glass of whiskey to steady his nerves before trying to sew shut Devon's stitches, which had re-opened. What had resulted was a yelling match between the two boys that paused on a note of terror as Molly came storming out of her bedroom in a facemask to see what all the fuss was about. The argument then shifted to whether or not 'green mud' actually did moisturize your face. Rather than getting in the middle of it all, Rae and Gabriel had sat quietly on the couch, watching and holding in their amusement as accusations and bits of green sludge flew around the room.

Things finally cooled off when Rae gave Devon a shot of morphine for the pain, and gave the remainder of Julian's drink to Molly to help calm her down. After that, it was nothing but a quick brawl over showers before the lights snapped off and the house settled down to sleep.

But not everyone was asleep, a fact that Rae discovered as she tiptoed across the living room a few hours later to get a glass of water from the kitchen.

Why am I even getting up to do this? she thought as she padded across the tile. *I could have just conjured this in my room. Yeah, but then Devon would have woken up and—*

It was then that she saw a pair of green eyes watching her.

"Gabriel!" she whispered, clutching her chest. "You scared me."

Julian was passed out on the couch next to him, an arm thrown haphazardly across his face, but Gabriel was sitting exactly where Rae had left him on the couch. She doubted he had slept at all. As his bright eyes studied her in the dark, she suddenly wished that she was wearing more than a pair of pajama shorts and a thin camisole. But for one of the first times ever, Gabriel wasn't leering at her body. In fact, he was gazing deep into her eyes with a very thoughtful expression on his face.

"Devon's a good guy," he said suddenly.

Her eyebrows shot to the ceiling. "Devon's a good guy?" she repeated sarcastically. "Are you drunk or something? Who am I talking to here?"

A faint smile flashed across his face, but he looked steadily into her eyes. There was something almost appraising about his expression, like he was considering something.

"I'm serious—he's one of the good ones. You all are."

Rae was surprised to be included in his assessment. Had he not thought so before?

"Um...thanks, I guess?" She phrased it as a question, giving him an inquisitive smile.

He chuckled softly, running his fingers back through his blond hair. "Sorry. I guess it's just been a long day."

Indeed, there was a note of weariness in his voice that Rae hadn't noticed before, along with a look of deep exhaustion beneath his lovely sparkling eyes.

After glancing at Julian to make sure he was still asleep, she settled tentatively beside Gabriel on the couch, curling her legs up beneath her and angling towards him. The mission had taken its toll on him just as it had on the others. But while she and her friends got through days like this by playfully bantering and leaning on each other—Gabriel didn't have anyone. She was pretty sure of it.

And he saved your life...

Her skin flushed pink as she dropped her eyes to the couch. She remembered every second in painful, terrifying detail. The way her heart had seized up as her fingers slipped away from Devon's. The feeling of sickening horror as she started to fall. And then the moment of blinding, exquisite relief as another strong hand latched onto hers.

"What's wrong?" he asked softly, misreading her expression.

"Nothing's wrong, I just..." she looked up quickly, then paused when she saw his face.

They stared at each other for a long moment. Then she took his hand.

"Thank you," she said quietly. "For catching me. I didn't say it before, but...thanks."

He didn't say anything. He just stared at their hands. Then, slowly, his fingers wrapped around hers.

"It felt like the right thing to do..." he murmured, almost in himself.

Wait ...what? She slowly pulled back her hand, and for the second time that night, she felt like she was falling. He stared steadily back—absurdly beautiful and unnervingly intent—until, finally, it was she who had to look away.

From the corner of her eye, she saw his shoulders drop half an inch. When he spoke, he almost sounded disappointed. But it wasn't at her; that was the strange thing. She might not understand it, but none of it was directed at her.

"You should get some rest, Rae." He twisted around so he was lying down himself, his blond hair fanning out around him like a halo. "It's going to be another long day tomorrow."

For a moment, she just stared. There was something about his words that chilled her skin, like he knew something she didn't. Like there was something else about to come.

Then Devon stirred in the next room, and she pushed to her feet. She forced a tight smile and bid him goodnight before disappearing back into her bedroom. As she settled down on the mattress beside him, Devon's arm automatically wound around her waist.

But for the first time, she took no comfort in the gesture. The warmth of his skin and the steady pulse of his heart did nothing to steady her nerves.

She wasn't sure anything could...

She couldn't remember falling asleep. She couldn't remember much of anything after she'd floated back to her room just a few hours before.

The morning sun made no sense to her.

Rae didn't need to guess what Molly was going to say a moment later when she burst into the room the next morning. She knew what had happened the second she heard the scream. Exactly what had happened.

"Gabriel's gone! He took the bloody brainwashing piece!"

"I told you, I didn't see a thing!" Julian exclaimed for the fifth time, wiping dried blood off his face. "The bastard knocked me out in my sleep. Must have known I would have seen when he decided to—"

"Why was it in *his* jacket?" Molly said accusingly.

"Why not?" Devon shot back, pacing angrily through the penthouse. "Carter trusted him, so we trusted him. He helped us break into the Privy Council, for crying out loud. We had no reason *not* to trust him." His face darkened menacingly. "I swear, when I get my hands on that piece of shit—"

"But why was it even in his jacket?" Molly insisted. "Rae's the one who recovered the piece."

"Because I gave it to him," Rae spoke up for the first time.

She remembered the look on Gabriel's face when she slipped the device through the bars; the way his eyes had flicked between it and her before he finally pocketed it and reached down to help. Why had he even bothered? He'd gotten what he came for.

"Jules, can you see anything yet?" Devon pressed, glancing at his watch. "Who knows how much of a head start he already has."

"I should have known," Rae said quietly.

Molly tossed her hair back dismissively. "Come on, Rae. How could you have known?"

"When I talked to him last night...something was off. I could feel it."

Devon paused mid-step, his eyes flashing uncertainly to her face "You talked to him last night?"

Rae shook her head, lost in thought. "Just for a minute. I was getting a glass of water from the kitchen and he was still awake." She played the whole thing back in her head, heart quickening as she glossed over certain parts. "There was just something...weird about him. He looked disappointed...I think it was with himself. Kept talking about what good people we were." She glanced up at Devon. "Said that you were a good guy."

Molly leaned over with her hands on her hips. "*That* didn't cue you in?"

"Come on, Molls. Lay off."

"He's going to the train station," Julian said with sudden authority, his eyes darkening from their opaque white. "And he's alone. If we leave now, we might be able to catch him."

They snatched up their coats and ran for the door, but even as they did a little voice kept nagging in the back of Rae's mind. *He knew Julian would eventually wake up and track him. If he was on the wrong side, why didn't he kill Julian in his sleep? Why just knock him out?* She was about to voice these concerns, but something about the look on Devon's face made her pause.

Instead, she kept silent while the four of them leapt into the car and headed to Waterloo Station.

Even with some supernatural help, they made it through the ticket barrier and onto the platform just as the train was pulling away.

"*Damn it!*" Devon cursed, startling several passing pedestrians. He folded his hands behind his head and stared at the departing train like he was seriously considering running it down.

"It's okay," Molly said quickly, "we'll just get him at the next stop. Jules, where is he going next?"

Julian's eyes went white, but Rae put a hand on his arm. "I don't think that's going to be necessary," she said.

The three of them followed her gaze and froze dead in their tracks.

Gabriel was sitting on a bench at the far end of the platform, staring at the departing train like he, too, couldn't believe he wasn't on it. Then, almost as if he could feel their eyes upon him, he turned slowly and met their gaze.

His shoulders rose and fell as he took a deep breath, and, without a word he pushed himself to his feet and started walking over.

"I'm going to kill him," Devon muttered, eyes locking on him with pure hatred. "I'm going to kill him right here in public."

Molly and Julian looked like they were right there with him, but Rae shook her head.

"Why didn't he get on the train?"

When Gabriel finally got close enough to hear, she repeated the question again.

"Why didn't you get on the train?"

For the first time since she'd met him, all the cocky arrogance was gone. The cool self-confidence had vanished with the train, and the young man standing in front of her looked as pale and lost as a child.

They locked eyes for the briefest of moments before he slowly shook his head.

"I...I don't know..."

Chapter 12

After all the years she had known him, Rae never knew Devon could hit so hard.

There was a sharp cry, and Gabriel spat a mouthful of blood onto the ground.

Devon stepped forward again and hissed, "Who do you work for! Is it the Privy Council? Or Cromfield?!"

Before Gabriel could answer, Devon hit him again. Rae turned away.

He had put up no fight at all at the train station, following along beside them with his mouth shut and Molly's electric little fingers placed firmly on his back. When they led him to the penthouse and tied him to a recliner, he'd said not a word. Even when they bound him there with rope and carefully removed all traces of metal from their clothing, he kept his silence.

To be honest, he looked as overwhelmed by the whole thing as they were, silently watching with wide eyes as they tightly strapped his arms and legs to the chair.

When they were finished, Devon and Julian stepped forward, while Molly and Rae took a deliberate step back.

Rae shook her head. "You boys have obviously done this sort of thing before."

"Twice," Julian had grimaced at the memory.

Molly shuddered and sat down silently on the other side of the room, covering her face with her hands as Devon hit Gabriel again and again.

"Cromfield," Gabriel gasped, when he was finally able to catch his breath. "I work for Cromfield. Not Carter—not the Privy Council. That was the cover. Cromfield wanted me on the inside." He eyed Devon's raised fist warily, but with the look of someone who wouldn't resist.

"And you give this information up so easily?" Devon shook his sore hand. "I don't believe you."

"I'll tell you whatever you want to know," Gabriel said and glanced at Rae as he said this last part.

She found she was having a hard time looking at his beautiful, bloodied face.

"I really wouldn't," Devon growled, stepping firmly in between them. "How long?"

Gabriel snapped his eyes back to his interrogator. "What?"

"How long have you been working for Cromfield? Did he just recruit you, or—"

"He didn't recruit me."

"You went willingly?" Molly shrieked.

"No!" Gabriel shook his head. "Since I was a kid, too little to remember when." Shallow, jerking breaths raised his shoulders quickly up and down. "That's how Cromfield recruits people—he does it when they're children. I was four or five."

For the first time, Devon paused. Julian's brow creased with forbidden sympathy, and Rae could tell he was thinking about Angel, but by the time he'd turned to Devon, Devon had already composed himself and was ready with the next question.

"So why did he send you here? *Be specific.*"

Rae shuddered at his tone. In all her years, she'd never heard Devon sound like that. She saw it now—why the Council had always considered him such a valuable resource, such a dangerous agent—the one tasked with the most lethal assignments. The valuable part, she'd understood immediately. Devon was strong, smart, and quick on his feet. But dangerous? As she watched him standing there, looming over Gabriel with a trail of blood dripping slowly down his fist, she realized that she had never once seen him as dangerous.

Until now.

"He knew you and Julian were the ones tasked with hiding the pieces of the device. He knew that if he stole one, Carter would eventually send you to collect the rest of them before he could do it first. And in doing so...he thought that you would find the last of the four, especially the one he was never able to locate himself."

"So he knew where the other two were this whole time? He's just been biding his time, letting us do the dirty work for him, before you delivered the device?"

"...that was the plan."

Devon raised his hand again, but Julian pushed him casually aside, squatting down in front of Gabriel's chair. "So what went wrong? Back at Guilder—the trip-wire. That was you, wasn't it?"

Rae looked up suddenly. She hadn't even made that connection.

Gabriel sighed. "Yeah, that was me. It wasn't that hard to do. When you left," he glanced at Devon, "there was a power vacuum amongst the agents. It's the reason I was able to rise to the top so fast. I bided my time, and it wasn't long before Carter began to trust me, confide in me, even. He started to leak me bits of information, which I kept to myself; I knew it was a test." He was speaking quickly now, in a soft, clipped monotone. It was as if the act of confessing was almost a relief to him. After all this time, all these secrets, he was finally free.

"Then one night, he called me into his office. After pouring me a drink, he told me all about your secret mission. About the hybrids and Cromfield and how he'd been trying to help you. He said you were coming back soon, and that Rae was going to be arrested. He asked me to break her out so you could continue on with your mission."

"Which you then told to Cromfield," Molly piped up from the corner. There was a dark look on her face that Rae had never seen before. It didn't really seem to fit.

"He was pleased," Gabriel said. There was a lifeless look about him whenever he mentioned Cromfield directly. A sort of shutting down that he had no control over. "I had placed myself in the perfect position to help you get the pieces, and then deliver them to him."

Julian hadn't moved an inch and his eyes bore into Gabriel's as he re-asked his question.

"So why the trip-wire?"

For the first time, Gabriel was uncertain. His eyes darted frantically around the room, before coming to rest ever so briefly upon Rae. Then his shoulders fell with a whispered sigh. "I wasn't supposed to do that," he confessed. His voice was so soft they could barely hear it, and although Rae didn't think he realized it himself, his hands had begun shaking. "Cromfield doesn't want Rae hurt. He never has. Quite the contrary, actually. But Rae..." When he looked up at Devon, his face actually grimaced into an ironic smile. "You say that Rae is your whole life...? Well, she was mine too."

Devon's hand flew back in the air, but Julian caught him by the wrist. "Hear what he has to say," he murmured.

But before Devon could answer, Rae pushed both boys out of the way and knelt down in front of Gabriel herself. Her eyes were stinging with angry, unshed tears as she stared him down. She didn't know why she was feeling this way. She'd been burned and betrayed by the people around her since she first stepped into this crazy world. But, for whatever reason, this one felt different. This one felt personal.

She had trusted him. She had...she had let him in.

"What the hell's that supposed to mean?" she demanded in a soft, lethal tone.

A hint of the hurt she was feeling herself flickered across Gabriel's face, but he checked himself quickly, staring at her instead with wide, wounded eyes. "You have no idea what it was like," he breathed, "growing up in your shadow. Cromfield was the only family I ever had. He was *everything* I knew. But he didn't need me. He didn't care whether I made it past my sixth birthday. No, the only thing he ever cared about was you."

He stared deep into Rae's eyes and she stared back, just as transfixed. She had heard glimmers of this before. Seen flashes of it in Angel's mind. But hearing Gabriel say it right to her face? She felt as though her heart was breaking.

"You were all he ever talked about, all I ever heard about. Day in, day out. Year after year. I was raised to be a tool, a simple tool whose sole purpose was helping him acquire you. After he did? Well, I'm sure he wouldn't have kept me around much longer."

Rae's heart was pounding in her chest as she leaned closer. The two of them were almost touching when she murmured, "So you put the trip-wire there..."

A bloody tear ran down his cheek.

"...to kill you."

The interrogation ended with those words.

Upon hearing them, Devon had broken a marble paperweight over Gabriel's head. At first they'd thought he was dead, but he had a pulse—faint but steady. That being said, it was unlikely he would be waking up any time soon.

That didn't stop Rae, however, from using Carter's tatù to break into his thoughts.

When she'd done this with other people, her friends in training, her mother to help her get her memories back, even to find out the extent of Jennifer's crimes, she'd always felt like an intruder. To glimpse a person's inner-most thoughts, to peer inside their soul... It was an invasion that was never to be taken lightly, and one that she'd never quite been able to reconcile.

Until now.

She felt strangely justified seeing into Gabriel's mind, even if he was passed out cold and had no idea she was doing it. The guy had tried to kill her. And he had done possibly irreparable harm to their cause. It was her duty to continue the interrogation, one-sided if necessary, and find out exactly what he was up to.

At least...that's what she told her friends.

But the truth was that *she* needed to know. How could he do that to her? Why did he change his mind? He had the piece, she was just dangling here, they were alone...

What had happened?

"Are you sure you want to do this?" Julian asked quietly, placing a gentle hand on her shoulder. "You know once you go in, there's no going back."

Rae nodded. "I'll be fine." She glanced up at Devon. "I promise."

But from the second she put her hands on Gabriel's face, she wasn't fine.

Not by a long shot.

No amount of training or steeling of will could have possibly prepared her for the tangle of emotions she saw just behind those sparkling eyes. This was a boy who had never known love, who had never known safety or real happiness. He was taught from a young age that he was *less*. Less than the man he worked for. Less than the girl he was being groomed to ensnare. And he believed it.

He hid it masterfully beneath a careful façade of supreme confidence. Eventually, confidence wasn't enough, and he got cocky. He trained harder and faster than anyone she'd ever seen in her entire life. Maybe if he did, Cromfield would finally take notice... finally see the worth in the little boy with the sad green eyes. But he never did. Years passed, and he never did.

Mixed in with the muddled flash of images, she saw a small white-haired girl that she had seen before. Angel. The love of Julian's life. Gabriel's only childhood companion.

Rae saw the look on Gabriel's face when she herself had called Cromfield to tell him that Angel was dead; she'd died by Rae's own hand. While Cromfield had been impassive, there was a cold fury on Gabriel's face, the likes of which she had never seen.

It was then that the visions started changing, taking on a secretive and sinister tone.

In Gabriel's mind—in his very heart—Rae was the bane of his entire existence. He didn't blame Cromfield; he couldn't. No matter how hard he tried to despise him, the second he saw his terrifying master, he was just a five-year-old boy again. So he turned his rage to Rae instead.

Cromfield needed her alive? Well, Gabriel needed her dead.

So he plotted and schemed. Waited until the right moment to strike. It would be at Guilder, he had decided. He would set another alarm. One they didn't know about. One that would isolate her from her friends while she was in a position of absolute vulnerability, with no tatùs.

He had been only mildly perturbed when he first met her. Did Cromfield ever say she was this beautiful? And funny! Besides Angel, he had never met a girl who could make him laugh. Yet the thing that had struck him most was her bravery. He had been forced into this tangled web of lies; he'd grown up without a choice. But Rae? She was choosing to fight it. Choosing to right the wrongs that had been done to her and her family.

And did he mention *beautiful*!? Did she have to be so —

But it didn't matter. Because she had to die.

So he waited for them to go after the second piece. He waited through the agonizing time in Scotland. Watching her from the corner of his eye. Warming when she came into a room. Aching to his very bones when he watched her interacting with friends and family, two constructs he knew absolutely nothing about but secretly craved. Then there was the strange hardening in his chest when he watched her smile at Devon, slip her hand into his.

After sleepless nights of wonder, he was finally able to identify it: jealousy.

But it didn't matter. Because she had to die.

When it was finally the night of the mission, the night they were to break into Guilder, he'd thought he was ready. He'd done nothing but force himself to actively hate her the entire night before. As he paced over the grass, heading to where he was supposed to meet her, he had fixed his mind on nothing but Angel—his only friend who this girl had killed in cold blood. He'd thought he was ready. He'd felt ready. He'd felt ready for anything. But all that changed the second he'd peered through the bars and saw her hanging there.

She was *crying*.

Rae gasped aloud as she felt what had passed through his heart in that moment. It was like it had split in two: the man he was, and the man he wanted to be.

She'd handed him the piece, and he'd thought to himself: this could be so easy. Just walk away, walk away and tell Cromfield she fell. He'd be punished, surely, but not blamed. Then maybe his life could start to be what it was always meant to. Then maybe, he could start anew.

Except...she was *crying*.

Before he knew what he was doing, he'd placed the piece into his jacket, and was working on breaking down the bars. When she'd slipped from Devon's hand, his own hand had flashed out of its own accord, holding on to hers as she dangled over the abyss.

What're you doing, Gabriel?! Let go!

But for the first time in his life, he couldn't. He held on like his own life depended on it.

After that, it had been time to leave. He was obviously in way over his head here and had no idea what he was doing. These were...these were good people.

Rae saw flashes of Molly giggling, Julian laughing with Devon, her own blue eyes...

How could hurting these people be the right thing to do? If these were the good guys, what exactly did that make him?

He'd decided to walk away, deliver the piece to Cromfield, and simply disappear. Yet Rae saw the hesitation in every step of the plan. The way his hands had hovered over Julian's throat before he simply knocked him out instead. The way he'd deliberately stopped from sabotaging their car to stop them from getting to the station on time. The way he'd watched the train pull slowly away from the platform...a single thought in his mind.

He wished he'd kissed Rae last night.

Rae pulled away with a gasp. A flood of tears poured down her face before she could stop them, and she found herself scrambling backwards, finally coming to a stop against the wall. Her friends stared at her with wide, worried eyes, and Devon took an automatic step forward.

"Sweetheart? What is it? What did you see?"

A rush of emotions coursed through her, all centered around one simple truth. But as her eyes travelled from Gabriel's sleeping body to Devon's worried face, she pushed them down. Down to the deepest part of her. Down so far that even she would never find them...

"He could have gone to Cromfield, but he stopped," she panted, trying to collect herself. "I think...I think he's wanted to get away for a long time—he just didn't know it yet himself. He doesn't know much about Cromfield's plans, though. His only purpose was to get the pieces of the device."

Devon was watching her carefully, his lovely eyes latched on to hers. He opened his mouth once to speak, but then thought better of it and took a seat on the sofa, turning to Julian instead.

Julian glanced at him in surprise but then started nodding quickly, trying to formulate some sort of plan. "Okay, so he doesn't want to go back to Cromfield. What do we do with him?

We can't bring him to the Privy Council. It's not like we can work with him, and we can't just let him go free—"

"No, that's *exactly* what we're going to do," Rae said firmly, forming a plan of her own. "But before we turn him loose, he'd going to deliver a little message for me. Right to his dear old bastard boss..."

"Wake up, Gabriel."

Some conjured smelling salts were waved under his face, but still he didn't budge.

"Come on, you bastard. Open your lousy freaking—oh, there you go. Good morning."

Gabriel blinked up at them in a daze, squinting in the bright sun. There were still dark smears of blood covering almost every inch of his face, and his eyes looked like they were in constant danger of closing.

"What..." he cleared his throat as his eyes focused, and tried again. "Why am—"

"You're still alive because, unlike you, we don't believe in killing people in cold blood," Molly said coolly, folding her arms across her chest.

"And because I obviously miscalculated with the paperweight," Devon mumbled.

"Because I need you to do something for me," Rae interjected.

Gabriel turned his eyes painfully to hers, and again she found she had to look away.

I'll never tell him, she decided on the spot. *I'll never tell anyone.*

Devon hadn't liked the idea of her plan, but she had seen over seventeen years' worth of Cromfield's intentions through Gabriel's eyes.

He didn't want to force her. He wanted her to choose.

And therein lay her only tactical advantage.

The message was simple, and was to be hand-delivered. She would not join him. She would never join him. She detested his very thought. In no alternate dimension, in no eternal amount of time, would she ever come round. *That* was her decision. Her final say.

This had been summarized very neatly in a letter which she now handed to Gabriel.

"I want you to give this to your old boss."

He looked down at it for a moment before taking it in a trembling hand. He seemed surprised that his arms were no longer bound, which he'd realized after he'd already reached.

"My...*old* boss?" he repeated, straining the operative word.

"Well," Molly said with a nasty smile, "we figure he's not exactly going to want you back after he learns you failed so miserably at your mission."

"No, probably not." Gabriel's gaze flicked to Rae before falling to the floor. "I could have run, but I didn't... I don't know why."

"You need to take this to him," Rae repeated, trying to keep her voice from wavering, "and then you're free to do as you please. Like Angel."

"You're free to get the hell out of here and never come back is what she means," Devon corrected.

"Unless Cromfield has something for me in return," Rae continued, "which I'm guessing—given the heated content of this letter—he actually might."

Gabriel stared at each of their faces in turn before looking back down at the letter. Rae didn't know if he realized it yet—she didn't think the others did either. The letter was her gift to him. A letter like that demanded a reply, and in doing so it would save Gabriel's life. Instead of being killed on the spot for failing to complete his task—he would get to come back.

If only for a little while...

"If you don't do it, Julian will track you down and I'll let Devon finish what he started." She said the words but didn't mean them. He was just another victim of Cromfield's games. *Like her father?*

"No," Gabriel said softly, pushing gingerly to his feet, "I'll do it." He wavered for a moment, reaching back to the chair for balance, until he recovered himself. Although the faces around him gave him no reprieve, he looked at each one again for a second more before landing on Rae's.

He didn't know what to say. She didn't either. Perhaps there was nothing to say.

Did he know? Could he know what she'd done? What she'd seen? She didn't think so. Then again, there was something about those sparkling eyes that made her pause. That had always made her pause.

"I'm sorry," he finally said. Short and flat. Almost cocky. As was his style.

Rae shrugged. "Don't be sorry. I won."

For a second, a hint of a smile lifted the corner of his lips. Then he grabbed up his coat and swept out of the apartment. Before they had a chance to change their minds.

Before she had a chance to say goodbye.

A soft knock on the door made her look up from the bed. She'd been sitting there the entire day, ever since Gabriel had left that morning, and graciously, everyone had given her some space. It was nighttime now, and she suspected that space had finally run out.

"Come in," she called.

The door opened and Devon walked inside. He was dressed to go out, holding her coat under one arm as he extended the other towards her.

"Will you come somewhere with me?" he asked quietly.

For a minute, she just stared. She didn't think she'd ever get used to it. Not in her entire, eternal life. The sight of him standing there in the lamplight.

Devon was...beautiful. There was no other word for it. But it wasn't just the look of his face that stopped her cold. It was the look *on* his face.

He loved her. Completely and utterly. With every bit of his heart.

It was enough to leave a girl speechless.

"Um...of course," she said, getting up. "And where might we be going?"

He smiled, holding up her coat as she slipped her arms inside. "It's a secret..."

They walked for about ten minutes, bundled and intertwined as they strolled around the edge of the little park that Rae's balcony looked across. Then, when they were several blocks down, Devon suddenly stopped. Rae came to a halt beside him, looking up at his face in surprise before following his line of sight to a little house that stood framed by some willows.

"What do you think?" he asked quietly.

Rae frowned slightly as she gazed up at the charming little cottage. "What is it?"

He gave her a quirky smile. "It's my house. Well, mine and Julian's."

There was a moment's pause."

"You *bought* a house?!" Rae exclaimed in alarm, looking back at it in a whole new way. "You freakin' over-achiever! I thought you guys were just renting an apartment like Molly and me."

He chuckled and stared up at it. "We were going to, but then I thought..." His voice trailed off, and for a second, he looked almost nervous. "You've always like this area, and..."

She squeezed his hand and caught his eye. "What is it? Tell me?"

"Rae," he took a deep breath, "I want to put down roots. I don't just want to rent an apartment. I want to build a life here...with you."

His eyes shone with sudden worry and she realized she'd stopped breathing. Of course, her super-human boyfriend could hear that.

"Sorry," she stammered, "I just, um..."

He took her hands. "I know our lives might not be what you'd call normal. Okay, I know they don't even come close. And maybe they never will, but...I love you, Rae Kerrigan. I have from the moment I laid eyes on you. From the moment I tackled you to the ground."

They both laughed lightly, remembering their awkward introduction.

"I have no idea where our lives are taking us," he said softly. "Right now, that seems more uncertain than it's ever been. But there is one thing I am certain about...and that's you. You will always have me. I will always love you. No matter how 'un-normal' our lives are, no matter what else gets thrown our way. That much will never change."

He might have been about to say more, but Rae would never know. Because at that moment, she couldn't stop herself from jumping into his arms and kissing him with all her might.

He was right. No matter what happened, or how muddied the waters got. He was hers and she was his. That was simply the way it was, the way it would always be.

When she pulled back a minute later, he was smiling.

"Ahhh... Is that what you said to Julian when you and he bought the house?" she teased gently.

The smile faded. "One moment I love you, and the next I want to kill you," he laughed and pulled her into a tight hug with his good arm.

Chapter 13

For the next few days Rae stressed, along with her three suitemates. Would Gabriel bring the letter to Cromfield? She wanted to hope, but the need to be realistic weighed heavy on her. What would Cromfield do when he read the note? Would he hurt Gabriel, or worse? Two long days of stress and worry.

Four teenagers hiding out in a decadent London penthouse without the opportunity to properly enjoy it.

Empty take-out boxes littered the floor. Empty coffee mugs filled the sink. They couldn't leave the apartment to pick up food. They were in the heart of London and there were too many people making too many minute-by-minute decisions for Julian to know whether or not they might be spotted. So they stayed inside and ordered take-out with delivery, using the luxury apartment as a safe-house. Hiding, pacing, and obsessively checking their phones.

In spite of the fact that they would most likely have to leave it behind forever, Molly actually started unpacking some of the boxes. The others didn't have the heart to tell her no, and before long they all found themselves starting to help. It was a good distraction—something to keep their heads and hands busy as they waited for the sky to fall.

By the morning of the third day, they had actually made great progress. There were paintings on the walls, carpets on the floor, utensils in the cabinets. The boys had driven themselves crazy trying to put together an apartment's worth of furniture. "*Some* assembly required..." Julian had cursed. A load of empty cardboard boxes lay stacked in a pile by the door, as, before long, most everything inside them had found itself a home.

It was a rather hilarious juxtaposition, Rae realized, as she stood back and admired the finished product. Her stuff versus Molly's. Although it had miraculously come together to look like what Molly called, 'the ultimate bachelorette pad,' it was easy to see what belonged to who.

Despite her vivacious personality, Molly was restrained elegance and class all the way. It didn't really matter whether or not she actually liked something—if it was expensive, she would buy it and mount it proudly on the walls: The unfortunate reason they had literally ended up with a pair of glass sitting chairs—a purchase Devon had 'accidently' broken to rescue Rae from having to say no.

As for Rae's things, they were a bit more on the whimsical side. Molly had politely tolerated her Tibetan prayer scarves, and Moroccan incense holders. Her mouth had thinned into a hard line, but she had forced it up into a smile when Rae hung a Gustav Klimt in the hallway. But when Rae had placed a turquoise papasan chair in the living room, Molly had zapped it without a word.

Somehow, while trying to distract themselves from Gabriel's non-return, they had found a delicate sort of equilibrium; a balance that came off as rather charming, Rae thought as she wandered distractedly over to answer the knock on the door.

"Jules, did you already order din—" She froze in place.

"What's up, gorgeous?"

Her mouth fell open in horror as her eyes swept over the man standing in front of her. At least what was left of him. "Gabriel..." she finally managed, "What the...?"

When they had released him, just three days before, he was admittedly a little worse for wear. Actually, he looked like he'd taken Carrie to the prom. Devon hadn't gone easy on him, and it would certainly have been a while until his face looked its normal gorgeous again.

But this...?

This was a whole other level.

Rae couldn't see a single part of him that wasn't hurt. Not an inch of his skin didn't appear bruised or battered. Every movement was an obvious effort. Even his eyes seemed to have lost their usual shine, but that was probably just because of the purple bruises around both of them.

He could still smile, though. And the second he saw her, a part of him lit up. "Oh, you know. Tripped down the stairs, mauled by a bear. Delivered the wrong kind of letter to my boss..." His grin faltered for a fraction of a second before returning in full force, re-opening a torn lip. "What about you? What've you been up to? Trying to stop the world from evil, plotting, psychotic bastards?"

Rae felt like she did the first time she'd ever been zapped by Molly. There was a sharp burning around her eyes, and a prickling sting that echoed through and through. "Are you really going to stand there and make small-talk right now?" she asked in disbelief. *How was he even standing?!*

He glanced surreptitiously around him with that same inexplicable grin. "Are you really going to leave someone who looks like the zombie apocalypse incarnate standing on your doorstep? Honestly, Kerrigan. What will the neighbors say?"

She grabbed his wrist and pulled him inside, just as the other three returned from where they had been hanging up drapes in the far bedroom.

"No, I didn't call it in," Julian answered Rae's question from moments before. "But if you're in the mood for..."

The three of them stopped dead in their tracks, their mouths falling open just like Rae's as they stared in open astonishment at Gabriel.

"What the...?" Molly's face paled in horror. "How did..."

It was amazing how casual Gabriel could look, even standing amongst the same people who had recently taken a vote to kill him. It was amazing how, still bloodied, he could manage to grin again. "Just had a nasty little run-in with karma, that's all. But I couldn't very well leave London without saying a proper goodbye." He rifled around for a moment in his jacket before pulling out a blood-smudged envelope. "And without giving you this."

"You were gone for three days," Rae blurted, completely ignoring the letter in his hands.

Gabriel rolled his eyes. "Look, if you wanted expedited shipping, you should have—"

"He kept you for *three whole days?* Doing this to you?" *Because we sent him there—because I sent him there.* She stared at him in utter horror. She had done this. To another human being.

Molly clapped her hands over her mouth as tears of horror sprang to her eyes. On her other side, Julian marched straight to the kitchen, looking a little sick. When he returned, he brought with him several clean towels and a bottle of rubbing alcohol.

Only Devon didn't move. He had been shocked like the rest, to see Gabriel bleeding a crimson pool into the new carpet. But after that he hadn't moved an inch. He just stared.

"What do you say, Dev?" Gabriel was still trying to grin, although it was getting almost painful just to watch. "How about while she reads it, you and I go for round two? No ropes this time."

Devon's eyes closed for a brief moment before he extended his hand. "Come on," he said quietly.

Gabriel's gaze flicked between his hand and his face before taking a step back. "Look, I was kidding. I delivered your damn letter—"

"Let's get you stitched back together and cleaned up."

Fixing Gabriel up was quick but brutal. It was something the boys took over while Molly and Rae hovered outside the bathroom door, trying not to cry. At one point, Devon called for Rae to give him a syringe of drugs to dull the pain. She instantly complied, peering past him as she handed it through the door.

Gabriel was sitting on the counter, half-slumped against the mirror with his eyes closed. It appeared that he had kept himself going just long enough to get to the house full of his enemies, and now he was spent. His shirt had been cut carefully off and was lying in tattered pieces on the floor, while Julian stood in front of him, pulling what looked like a piece of glass from his side.

"Hey," Devon murmured, soft enough that only the two of them could hear, "he's going to be alright. Nothing we're seeing is bad enough to kill him."

Unable to speak, Rae just shook her head, a fresh wave of tears pouring down her face.

"Rae," he caught her gently by the shoulder, unintentionally staining her shirt with a smear of blood, "he's safe now. He's with us."

He's with us.

The words echoed back to her a million times as the sun travelled slowly across the sky before settling down behind the trees.

A part of her rejected the notion flat-out. He was not *with* them. He couldn't be. For so very many reasons. But another part embraced the thought as soon as the words were said. Because no matter how strange or unbelievable...they were quite simply the truth.

Too many people had already died in this useless war. A secret war with no clear enemy, just a host of invisible dangers and heartbreaking casualties. Rae had lost people on both sides, and gained people too. She had risen and fallen with the tide.

And then there was Gabriel...

Despite all his bravado, Gabriel was a casualty too. He had been since he was just a kid of five years old. He, Angel, Jennifer, even her terrifying half-brother Kraigan. They were all victims too. Victims of manipulation, victims of circumstance, victims of tragedy and force. There was no one on either side who hadn't been touched by the darkness of a single man.

A man everyone had once said was her father. Except she knew the truth, even when nobody would believe her—Simon Kerrigan was a victim too.

Gabriel was with them now because they all had to stand together. If they didn't, they wouldn't stand a chance.

Rae snapped out of her dark introspection as the door to the bathroom opened and closed behind her. Devon and Julian stepped out, carrying Gabriel in between the two of them and setting him gently down on the couch. He was fast asleep.

Molly walked forward the next second and covered him in a blanket that Rae recognized as being from her friend's own bed. After propping an extra pillow beneath his head, she took a seat on the floor in front of him and pulled out a book, positioning herself like a casual sentry as the boys did the same thing unconsciously on either side. None of them seemed to think about it, this protective behavior, and watching them, Rae couldn't help but smile as she moved behind the couch to stand behind Gabriel.

Yes, whether she liked it or not, Gabriel was certainly with them now.

He awoke only once in the night, bolting upright and staring around as if coming to from a nightmare. His eyes widened in confusion when he saw the three of them sleeping around him, and widened some more when Rae leaned over to him in the dark.

"Shhh." She put her finger over her lips. "It took forever for them to fall asleep."

Again, Gabriel stared around, not understanding. "I don't remember what—"

"We gave you some drugs to help with the pain," she explained gently as she moved and perched on an armrest beside him. Devon twitched in his sleep, but did not wake, and the rest of them were out cold. "Here," she conjured another dose, "this should help take the edge off."

She offered it, but Gabriel just stared at her, looking almost wary.

"Why're you helping me?" he finally asked.

Their eyes locked and she gave him a gentle smile. "Because you helped me. Whatever you did before—you saved my life, Gabriel. And then almost lost your own. You're one of us now."

He took a second to absorb this before glancing around at the sleeping friends, assessing them in a whole new light. Then he took the syringe from Rae's hand. Without a bit of hesitation, he stuck it into the crook of his elbow and closed his eyes as the medication flowed through his veins.

When he slowly opened his eyes again, he was visibly relaxed, staring at Rae with a dazed, vaguely familiar, cocky smile. "That's...good to know."

She laughed silently, stroking back his hair without thinking about it. "Yeah, well, for us too. Not only did you make a terrible enemy, but I'm afraid we're going to need all hands on deck in the days ahead. You might not like what you've signed on for."

"It comes with perks." He grinned, laying his head back on the pillow. "I'm looking at one of them..."

Rae's eyes flickered automatically to Devon before she shook her head with a rueful smile. "Really? He just spent the entire day stitching you up and you're going to do that right now?"

"What can I say?" He shrugged slightly. "It's the drugs talking."

They both grinned at each other.

"But seriously, Rae...it's good to know." Without him seeming to notice, his fingers started tracing hers, skating lightly across and drawing absentminded shapes.

It's the drugs talking. She casually pulled away and got to her feet. "Goodnight, Gabriel."

"Goodnight." He leaned back with a tired but content sigh as she made her way to her room. She had almost reached the door when he called again in a whisper only she'd be able to hear. "Rae?"

There was still a slight smile on his face, but his eyes were clear and focused as they locked on hers in the dark.

"I know what you did."

Her heart stopped in her chest. A wave of panic rushed up from her toes, and she hastened to turn her look of terror into a polite frown. "Excuse me?"

His eyes twinkled.

"I know what you saw."

"What? I mean, no. Impossible. I don't know what you're—" But she might as well have saved her denial. As soon as he'd said the words, the drugs took hold, and Gabriel fell into the most peaceful of sleep.

"You need to read it."

Rae shook her head, staring across the counter at the bloody envelope. "I don't even want to. What good will it do?" Her eyes flicked to Gabriel, still sleeping on the couch. "And at what cost?"

"Do you want me to read it for you?" Molly pressed, leaning over her cup of coffee.

Both girls had woken up at the crack of dawn and had stumbled upon the letter from opposite sides of the kitchen at the same time. In the trauma of everything that had happened yesterday, the actual purpose for Gabriel's visit and subsequent beating had been forgotten.

"You need to read it," Molly said again, following her gaze. "You owe him that."

Rae sighed and picked it up with delicate fingers, holding it briefly in her hands.

One lousy piece of paper. That's what Gabriel almost lost his life for.

Pulling in a deep breath, she sliced open the top and removed the letter, smoothing it down on the counter before she read:

My dear, sweet Rae,

I see you uncovered my assistant. Clever girl. I was very sorry to have to manipulate you in any way, but extreme times call for extreme measures. I'm sending what's left of him back to you, for you to do with as you please. He's of no further use to me.

I was also very sorry to read the letter you sent. I had hoped that after witnessing the treachery of your own Council, after seeing the potential in so many hybrids, your eyes might be opening to the light. But the fault lies with me. I can see now that I have pushed you too fast, too hard.

You see, my darling girl, there is no 'saying no' to me. There is no resisting. You and I were gifted with everlasting life, and therefore our union is only a matter of time. This truth, however, is something you have to come to on your own terms, in your own time.

Fortunately, time is something of which we are eternally assured. And if time is something you need, then I will give it to you. I'll not be attempting to interfere in your life again. Not until you're ready. If normalcy is what you desire, then by all means, follow your heart. I know where it will eventually lead. And I will be patiently waiting.

Until we speak again,

J. Cromfield

She and Molly looked at each other in disgust as the boys began to slowly stir. Rae's eyes rested on each one of them for a moment before stopping on Gabriel.

Cromfield had done that to Gabriel.

A man who had been slowly ruining their lives.

A man who the Privy Council refused to believe was alive.

That was about to change.

"Good morning," Devon murmured, stretching out his arms as he walked over before pulling her in for a quick kiss. Then his eyes fell on the letter lying between them, and his whole face darkened. "What did it say?" he asked nervously. "What did he tell you?"

Molly glanced at Rae before answering tentatively, "It...might have been almost good news?" She phrased it as a question. "I mean, he said he was going to leave her alone. Give her time to live a normal life before... let's just focus on that first part, I guess. He's backing off."

"Yeah—but we aren't," Rae said softly, her eyes burning a hole in the letter.

"Honey, please. I know that look," Devon pleaded. "Whatever it is you're planning, let's just tone it down a couple hundred degrees."

Her eyes flashed as she shot him a sudden grin. "Oh, babe, I think by now you know me better than that..."

Chapter 14

A nervous aide rushed down the hall and knocked hesitantly on the door to the president's office. He had only spoken to Carter once by himself, and he found the man overwhelmingly intimidating on a good day. He didn't exactly know how he was going to say this to him now.

"Come in," Carter barked.

Security had been heightened since the recent break-in, and the adjustment was still setting everyone on edge. The aide pushed his way inside past two hulking guards, and stood nervously in the center of the office. It took a second for Carter to look up from his papers to see what was taking so long.

"Speak," he demanded.

"Um, sir, I don't really know how to say this..."

Carter shot him a dry glare. "Why don't you try?"

"Well, you see, sir... There's a Rae Kerrigan at the front gate to see you."

The two men stared at each other for a long time before Carter buried his face in his hands. "Of course there is."

Five minutes later, Rae, Devon, Julian, and Molly stepped into the office, surrounded on all sides by heavily-armed guards. Rae had flat-out begged the others to stay behind with Gabriel—who was in no state to move—but they had just as firmly insisted they all come along.

"We're in this together," Molly had said, pulling on her coat. "You said it yourself."

"Besides," Devon winked, "how are we ever going to get that quasi-normal life I promised if we don't get this taken care of first?"

And so the four of them surrendered at the gates of Guilder; they had just one request. A request that was more of a demand the way Rae phrased it: to plead their case before the Council.

"Miss Kerrigan," Carter greeted her stiffly as the same crowd of men she'd seen just a few days before flooded into the room, parting around her like she was contagious. "I hope you know what you're doing here..."

Rae steadily held his gaze. 'Something that should've been done a long time ago."

The room settled down quickly with old snake-eyes, a man she thought Carter had called Victor, bringing up the rear. He fastened his colorless eyes upon her face as he sank down into a chair, staring as if he could obliterate her on the spot through nothing but force of will.

"Gentlemen," she said once they were all settled, her voice ringing loud and clear, "thank you for coming. I'm sorry to have...summoned you, but seeing as how the lot of you has interfered in my life many times over the last few years, I felt I was owed."

"Remember what we said about being respectful," Devon muttered behind her.

She resisted a smile, but sarcastically indulged him. "My *esteemed* members of the Privy Council," she threw down the letter on the table before them, "that letter was delivered to me yesterday morning. It's from Jonathon Cromfield."

There was a split second delay, like the room was waiting for the sound to catch up, before they erupted in unison, "That's utterly ridiculous—"

"Impossible!"

"We should just arrest her and be done with it."

"Carter, what's the meaning of—"

Rae raised her hand to silence everyone in the room. "I saw him in a vision, murdering my father and kidnapping my mother. I've met his associates—people raised their entire lives in his cult of terror. I've found his secret hiding place, under the catacombs of St. Stephen's Church right here in London. I've talked to him on the phone." She paused for effect. "*He is alive,* gentlemen. And I know what he's after."

Victor turned slowly in his chair to face Carter.

"James," he was the only one Rae had ever heard call Carter that besides her mom, "as acting president of this organization, it is your duty to stop this lunacy before it continues a second longer. The girl has clearly come unhinged—just like her father—and has already started to take your agents down with her. To claim that this man, who lived hundreds of years, ago could possibly be—"

"He *is* alive," Carter interrupted him softly, "I've seen him as well."

Rae blinked in astonishment, and for the first time felt a surge of hope. She had done this very much without Carter's permission, and had had no idea whether he would go along with it or not.

But apparently he had made his decision as well.

This time, instead of exploding into noise, the room went dead quiet.

Rae might be a 'crazy Kerrigan,' but Carter's word was above reproach. To hear him suddenly supporting her...what did it mean?

Victor's eyes flashed. "You can't be serious."

"I have never been more serious about anything in my life." Carter got slowly to his feet. "I've had my suspicions for some time about dark forces infiltrating this Council. We've had our share of leaks over the years. It is to be expected with an organization operating with such a reach, but since Miss Kerrigan has come of age and entered Guilder, the coincidences have become too many to ignore. Lanford. Kraigan. Miss Jones. In every scenario—Miss Kerrigan was a target."

"But you just said it yourself!" Victor exclaimed. "All these dark coincidences started happening the day *Miss Kerrigan* arrived at Guilder!"

"What are you suggesting, Victor?" Carter asked softly. "That Miss Kerrigan repeatedly attacked herself? Killed her own father when she was a toddler? Kidnapped her mother? Miss Kerrigan is not the enemy here. I tried to get you all to realize that by urging the Council to hire her on as an agent. To let her prove herself to you once and for all. But there is a force at play here that goes far beyond Miss Kerrigan. And yes, I'm referring to Jonathan Cromfield."

"It's simply not possible," another man spoke up from the end of the table. "Cromfield died years ago. How could he still be influencing changes now?"

"Because he's immortal, just like me," Rae interjected, bringing the attention of the room back to her. "Because he's a *hybrid*, just like me."

Another murmur went through the group, but this time she stared them down coldly, remembering the faces of each and every one of the hybrids Cromfield was trying to kill.

"He's been tracking them down—harvesting them for their powers, containing it in some kind of serum. For the month after graduation, my friends and I were trying to get to them first—to warn them to run for their lives." Her eyes narrowed. "Something we wouldn't have had to do if they weren't already on the run to begin with. *That's* what we've been doing. Running all over the world, fighting your battles for you. And for what? So I can come home and be arrested?"

She slowly shook her head, and for the first time she thought she saw scattered flashes of guilt. A few of the men at the table still refused to meet her eyes, but a few of them were looking at her with an honest streak of remorse. Some simply look baffled by the whole proceeding.

"And what about the device?!" Victor jumped to his feet. "You stole it from this very—"

It fell between them on the table with a loud clang.

"Only because Cromfield was going to steal it first. He'd already recovered one of the pieces, so again, my friends and I went to work gathering up the others...to *protect* them. To *protect* you."

She grabbed the other piece from Molly and threw it onto the table along with the first. The entire Council was silent as a grave, watching, but they were on the edge of their seats. This was proof. Proof of her innocence. Proof of her trust. Even if it was entirely undeserved.

Even if it was entirely broken.

"Hear this now because I'm only going to say it once: I am not my father."

Across the table, Carter nodded his head, beaming.

"This is my father's work—the entire culmination of his life. I'm handing it over to you. Because, despite what some of you will think, despite what I've been fighting to overcome since the day I set foot at your school, I'M NOT SIMON KERRIGAN!"

The relief of finally shouting the words was so strong, she could have cried. How long had she been waiting to say them? How long had they been weighing her down?

"I'm not something to be feared or kept in a dark cell—I have never, in my entire life, done anything at all but protect you people; protect you from the outside world, protect you from monsters that have infiltrated your very organization. Well, no longer."

In a blur of speed, all of the ten guards flanking them fell to the ground. Not hurt, but stunned. Curtesy of a fallen Angel.

"If you think I'm going back under arrest, you're crazy. And if you think I'm coming back to work for you, you're crazy too. I'm not sure what I'm going to do yet. I'm not on anyone's side anymore. I'm on my own side. I'm going to stop this lunatic before he kills one more innocent person. And I'm going to live my life free to make my own choices. Free from him. Free from you."

Without another word, she turned and walked out the door.

She thought maybe they were going to have to run. Maybe the entire speech would be for nothing, and the second it was finished the entire Council would close in on them and place them all under permanent arrest.

But they didn't. And the four friends walked out into the sunset of their own free will.

They could hear the aftermath of Rae's speech as they headed across the Guilder grounds. The very foundations of the Privy Council began to splinter and re-adjust as the world in which it operated was challenged to the core. But for once, Rae and her friends didn't care.

They simply continued walking until they had stepped outside the gates. Once there, they paused at the top of the drive, gazing out at the setting sun.

"I don't know what comes next," Rae said softly, staring out towards the horizon.

A soft breeze blew between them, stirring back their hair as they braced themselves for whatever was to happen next.

"I don't know either." Devon took her hand. "But we'll figure it out. Together."

It was dark by the time they touched back down in Scotland. The four of them had stayed very close together on the journey over, not saying much, just taking comfort in the proximity as they made their way slowly back to the house.

Beth was already waiting, her anxious face framed in the window as they pulled their rental car into the drive. Carter must have called her and told her what happened. Rae took a deep breath, slipping her hand back into Devon's as the four of them trudged up the gravel path to the house.

Would her mom be angry with her? Furious even? She certainly had every right to be. Not only had Rae risked re-arrest by returning to Guilder, but she had laid open every plan, placed every card on the table for all the world to see.

She happened to think that was a good thing. But her mom...? She wasn't so sure...

"Hey," she said tentatively as they stepped into the warm kitchen. "So I'm sure Carter's already called and told you the whole thing, but—"

"Honey," Beth interrupted, "there's going to be time for all of that and more later, I promise. But right now...well I'm afraid there's someone you need to see."

Rae glanced at her friends, but they looked just as bewildered as she did.

What in the world could possibly be more important than what they'd come to say?

"Oh come on, Beth," a deep voice said from the corner of the kitchen. "Why wouldn't she be happy to see me?"

Rae stomach dropped to the floor as Kraigan walked forward into the light.

"I am her brother, after all..."

THE END
MARK of FATE
Coming March 2016

After saying goodbye to the Privy Council, Rae Kerrigan thought the bulk of her troubles would be over. But as it turned out, they were just getting started...

She returns to her mother's house only to find her crazy half-brother Kraigan, who had followed the trail of an old enemy—Jennifer Jones. In the midst of gearing up for one of the biggest fights of her life, Rae finds herself at a series of crossroads—caught between two different futures, and two different men. As if that wasn't enough, a secret clue left by her father sends her on another adventure that only leads to more questions.

Will it be the Privy Council? Or a normal life in London?

Will it be Gabriel? Or will it be Devon?

She has to decide fast. Especially when it turns out Devon has a secret of his own...

Sneak Peek

Note from Author

Thanks for reading (and hopefully enjoying Twisted Together)! I'm still so enjoying how this story is playing out. I love writing about Rae's adventures, her friends and her life! I hope you guys don't mind sticking around for a few more rounds with Rae!

All the best, W.J. May

Newsletter: http://eepurl.com/97aYf

Website: http://www.wanitamay.yolasite.com

Facebook: https://www.facebook.com/pages/Author-WJ-May-FAN-PAGE/141704426081-49

The Chronicles of Kerrigan

Book I - *Rae of Hope* is FREE!
  Book Trailer:
  http://www.youtube.com/watch?v=gILAwXxx8MU
  Book II - *Dark Nebula*
  Book Trailer:
  http://www.youtube.com/watch?v=Ca24STi_bFM
  Book III - *House of Cards*
  Book IV - *Royal Tea*
  Book V - *Under Fire*
  Book VI - *End in Sight*
  Book VII – *Hidden Darkness*
  Book VIII – *Twisted Together*
  COMING FEBRUARY 19, 2016
  PREQUEL – Christmas Before the Magic

CoK Prequel!

A Novella of the Chronicles of Kerrigan.
A prequel on how Simon Kerrigan met Beth!!
AVAILABLE:
.99 cents for a Limited Time!

More books by W.J. May

Hidden Secrets Saga:
Download Seventh Mark part 1 For FREE
Book Trailer:

http://www.youtube.com/watch?v=Y-_vVYC1gvo

Like most teenagers, Rouge is trying to figure out who she is and what she wants to be. With little knowledge about her past, she has questions but has never tried to find the answers. Everything changes when she befriends a strangely intoxicating family. Siblings Grace and Michael, appear to have secrets which seem connected to Rouge. Her hunch is confirmed when a horrible incident occurs at an outdoor party. Rouge may be the only one who can find the answer.

An ancient journal, a Sioghra necklace and a special mark force life-altering decisions for a girl who grew up unprepared to fight for her life or others.

All secrets have a cost and Rouge's determination to find the truth can only lead to trouble...or something even more sinister.

RADIUM HALOS - THE SENSELESS SERIES
Book 1 is FREE:

Book Blurb:

Everyone needs to be a hero at one point in their life.

The small town of Elliot Lake will never be the same again.

Caught in a sudden thunderstorm, Zoe, a high school senior from Elliot Lake, and five of her friends take shelter in an abandoned uranium mine. Over the next few days, Zoe's hearing sharpens drastically, beyond what any normal human being can detect. She tells her friends, only to learn that four others have an increased sense as well. Only Kieran, the new boy from Scotland, isn't affected.

Fashioning themselves into superheroes, the group tries to stop the strange occurrences happening in their little town. Muggings, break-ins, disappearances, and murder begin to hit too close to home. It leads the team to think someone knows about their secret - someone who wants them all dead.

An incredulous group of heroes. A traitor in the midst. Some dreams are written in blood.

Shadow of Doubt
Part 1 is FREE!

Book Trailer:
http://www.youtube.com/watch?v=LZK09Fe7kgA

Book Blurb:

What happens when you fall for the one you are forbidden to love?

Erebus is a bit of a lost soul. He's a guy so he should be out to have fun but unlike the rest of his kind, he is solemn and withdrawn. That is, until he meets Aurora, a law student at Cornell University. His entire world is shaken. Feelings he's never had and urges he's never understood take over. These strange longings drive him to question everything about himself

When a jealous ex stalks back into his life, he must decide if he is willing to risk everything to be with Aurora. His desire for her could destroy her, or worse, erase his own existence forever.

Courage Runs Red
The Blood Red Series
Book 1 is FREE

What if courage was your only option?

When Kallie lands a college interview with the city's new hotshot police officer, she has no idea everything in her life is about to change. The detective is young, handsome and seems to have an unnatural ability to stop the increasing local crime rate. Detective Liam's particular interest in Kallie sends her heart and head stumbling over each other.

When a raging blood feud between vampires spills into her home, Kallie gets caught in the middle. Torn between love and family loyalty she must find the courage to fight what she fears the most and possibly risk everything, even if it means dying for those she loves.

Daughter of Darkness
Victoria

Only Death Could Stop Her Now
The Daughters of Darkness is a series of female heroines who may or may not know each other, but all have the same father, Vlad Montour.
Victoria is a Hunter Vampire

Free Books:

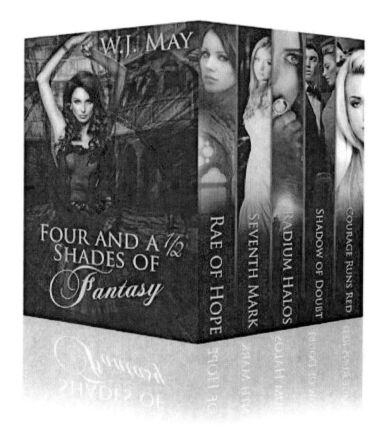

Four and a Half Shades of Fantasy

TUDOR COMPARISON:

Aumbry House——A recess to hold sacred vessels, often found in castle chapels.

Aumbry House was considered very special to hold the female students - their sacred vessels (especially Rae Kerrigan).

Joist House——A timber stretched from wall-to-wall to support floorboards.

Joist House was considered a building of support where the male students could support and help each other.

Oratory——A private chapel in a house.

Private education room in the school where the students were able to practice their gifting and improve their skills. Also used as a banquet - dance hall when needed.

Oriel——A projecting window in a wall; originally a form of porch, often of wood. The original bay windows of the Tudor period. Guilder College majority of windows were oriel.

Rae often felt her life was being watching through one of these windows. Hence the constant reference to them.

Refectory——A communal dining hall. Same termed used in Tudor times.

Scriptorium——A Medieval writing room in which scrolls were also housed.

Used for English classes and still store some of the older books from the Tudor reign (regarding tatùs).

Privy Council——Secret council and "arm of the government" similar to the CIA, etc... In Tudor times, the Privy Council was King Henry's board of advisors and helped run the country.

Don't miss out!

Click the button below and you can sign up to receive emails whenever W.J. May publishes a new book. There's no charge and no obligation.

Did you love *Twisted Together*? Then you should read *Four and a Half Shades of Fantasy* by W.J. May!

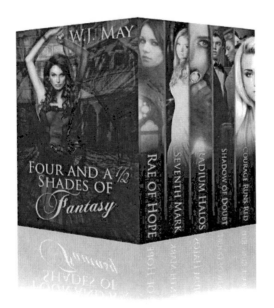

Four (and a half) Fantasy/Romance first Books from five different series! From best-selling author, W.J. May comes an anthology of five great fantasy, paranormal and romance stories. Books included: Rae of Hope from The Chronicles of Kerrigan Seventh Mark - Part 1 from the Hidden Secrets Saga Shadow of Doubt - Part 1 Radium Halos from the Senseless Series and an excerpt from Courage Runs Red from the Red Blood Series

Also by W.J. May

Bit-Lit Series
Lost Vampire
Cost of Blood
Price of Death

Blood Red Series
Courage Runs Red
The Night Watch
Marked by Courage

Daughters of Darkness: Victoria's Journey
Huntress
Coveted (A Vampire & Paranormal Romance)
Victoria

Hidden Secrets Saga
Seventh Mark - Part 1
Seventh Mark - Part 2
Marked By Destiny
Compelled
Fate's Intervention
Chosen Three

The Chronicles of Kerrigan
Rae of Hope
Dark Nebula
House of Cards
Royal Tea
Under Fire

End in Sight
Hidden Darkness
Twisted Together

The Chronicles of Kerrigan Prequel
Christmas Before the Magic

The Hidden Secrets Saga
Seventh Mark (part 1 & 2)

The Senseless Series
Radium Halos
Radium Halos - Part 2
Nonsense

The X Files
Code X
Replica X

Standalone
Shadow of Doubt (Part 1 & 2)
Five Shades of Fantasy
Glow - A Young Adult Fantasy Sampler
Shadow of Doubt - Part 2
Four and a Half Shades of Fantasy
Full Moon
Dream Fighter
What Creeps in the Night
Forest of the Forbidden
HuNted
Arcane Forest: A Fantasy Anthology
Ancient Blood of the Vampire and Werewolf

CPSIA information can be obtained
at www.ICGtesting.com
Printed in the USA
LVOW10s1559311017

554455LV00011B/1074/P